The Power Brokers

Political, Volume 4

Nicholas Andrew Martinez

Published by Harmony House Publishing, 2024.

This is a work of fiction. Similarities to real people, places, or events are entirely coincidental.

THE POWER BROKERS

First edition. November 24, 2024.

Copyright © 2024 Nicholas Andrew Martinez.

ISBN: 979-8230763529

Written by Nicholas Andrew Martinez.

Table of Contents

Chapter 1: The New Candidate 1
Chapter 2: The Hidden Agenda 8
Chapter 3: Allies and Enemies 14
Chapter 4: The Media War 22
Chapter 5: Secrets and Lies 29
Chapter 6: The Turning Point 36
Chapter 7: Betrayal 43
Chapter 8: The Scandal 49
Chapter 9: The Grassroots Movement...55
Chapter 10: The Threat 64
Chapter 11: The Conspiracy Unveiled 71
Chapter 12: The Assassination Attempt...77
Chapter 13: The Showdown 84
Chapter 14: The Collapse 91
Chapter 15: The New Era 102

To those who dare to challenge the status quo, who stand firm against corruption and fight for justice. Your courage paves the way for a better future.

And to the tireless activists, journalists, and everyday heroes who believe in the power of integrity and truth. This story is for you.

May we all find the strength to uphold our principles and inspire change.

Chapter 1: The New Candidate

David Collins stood on the steps of City Hall, the historic building's imposing façade serving as the backdrop to his announcement. The afternoon sun cast a golden glow over the crowd gathered before him, their faces filled with anticipation and curiosity. Cameras flashed, reporters murmured among themselves, and a palpable sense of expectancy hung in the air. Today marked the beginning of a new chapter, not only for David but for the entire city.

David was in his early thirties, with a charismatic presence that seemed to command attention effortlessly. His piercing blue eyes scanned the crowd, making brief but meaningful eye contact with as many people as he could. His tailored navy suit fit him perfectly, emphasizing his athletic build and adding to his aura of confidence and competence. Yet, it was his genuine smile and the sincerity in his voice that truly captivated those around him.

"Thank you all for being here today," David began, his voice steady and clear. "I stand before you not just as a candidate, but as a fellow citizen who believes in the potential of our great city. For too long, we've seen corruption and self-interest dominate our political landscape. It's time for a change. It's time for us to take back our city and create a government that truly serves its people."

Applause erupted from the crowd, and David took a moment to let their support wash over him. He had always known he was destined for something greater, something that would allow him to make a real difference. This candidacy was his chance.

David's journey to this moment had been anything but straightforward. Raised in a working-class neighborhood, he had witnessed firsthand the struggles and injustices that many people faced daily. His parents, both school teachers, had instilled in him a strong sense of justice and a desire to help others. David excelled academically, earning scholarships that took him to prestigious universities where he studied political science and law. He had spent years working as a public defender, fighting for those who couldn't fight for themselves, and later as an advocate for various social causes.

But despite his impressive resume and genuine passion for reform, David knew he needed more than just a good heart and a strong will to succeed in the cutthroat world of politics. That's where the Power Brokers came in.

The Power Brokers were a shadowy group of influential individuals who operated behind the scenes, shaping political landscapes to suit their interests. Their power and reach were vast, spanning across industries and governments. They had approached David months ago, recognizing his potential and offering their support. It was a tempting offer, one that came with resources, connections, and an almost guaranteed path to victory. But it also came with strings attached, and David was acutely aware of the potential compromises he might have to make.

"Today, I am announcing my candidacy for Mayor," David declared, the words feeling both thrilling and daunting as they left his lips. The crowd cheered louder, and David could see the hope in their eyes. They were ready for change, and he was ready to lead them.

After the speech, David mingled with the crowd, shaking hands and listening to their concerns. He made a point to remember names and faces, understanding that personal connections were crucial in building trust and support. As he moved through the throng, he felt a tap on his shoulder. Turning, he saw a familiar face – James Whitaker, one of the key members of the Power Brokers.

"David, a word?" James said, his tone friendly but insistent. He was a tall, imposing man in his mid-fifties, with sharp features and a calculating gaze.

"Of course, James," David replied, following him to a quieter corner of the plaza.

James looked around to ensure they were out of earshot before speaking. "That was a great speech, David. You've got the crowd eating out of your hand. But remember, this is just the beginning. The real work starts now."

David nodded, aware of the weight of responsibility that came with the Power Brokers' support. "I understand. And I appreciate everything you and your colleagues are doing to help me. But I want to make one thing clear – my goal is to serve the people, not the interests of a few."

James smiled, but it didn't quite reach his eyes. "Of course, David. We want the same thing. A strong, successful administration benefits everyone. Just remember, it's a delicate balance. We scratch your back, you scratch ours."

David forced a smile, knowing that this was the bargain he had struck. "I understand, James. I'll do my best to find that balance."

As James walked away, David couldn't shake the feeling that he was walking a tightrope. He believed in his vision for reform, but he also knew that he was playing a dangerous game. The Power Brokers had the power to make or break his career, and he had to navigate their demands carefully while staying true to his principles.

The weeks that followed were a whirlwind of campaign events, meetings, and strategy sessions. David's team, composed of passionate volunteers and seasoned political operatives, worked tirelessly to build his platform and spread his message. They crafted policy proposals that addressed the city's most pressing issues – corruption, education, healthcare, and infrastructure. They reached out to community leaders, organized rallies, and used social media to connect with voters.

David's popularity surged, and it became clear that he was a serious contender. His message of integrity and reform resonated with a populace tired of the status quo. But with success came increased scrutiny. The media began to dig into his past, searching for any skeletons in his closet. His opponents, threatened by his rise, launched smear campaigns and attacked his character.

Through it all, David remained focused. He knew that staying true to his vision and maintaining his integrity were paramount. He relied on his inner circle – trusted advisors like Rachel, his campaign manager, and Tom, his chief strategist – to navigate the political minefield.

One evening, after a particularly grueling day of campaigning, David sat in his modest campaign office, reviewing notes for an upcoming debate. Rachel walked in, her usually cheerful demeanor replaced by a look of concern.

"David, we need to talk," she said, closing the door behind her.

"What's wrong?" David asked, setting down his notes.

Rachel took a deep breath. "We've received information that the Power Brokers are planning to push through a controversial land development deal if you win. It's a project that's been in the works for years, and it involves displacing hundreds of low-income families. They're expecting you to support it."

David's heart sank. This was exactly the kind of situation he had feared. "I can't support that, Rachel. It goes against everything I stand for."

"I know," Rachel said, her voice softening. "But we need to be smart about this. We can't afford to alienate the Power Brokers right now. Maybe there's a way to negotiate, to find a solution that minimizes the impact on those families."

David nodded, appreciating Rachel's pragmatism. "I'll think about it. But I won't compromise my principles. There has to be another way."

That night, David couldn't sleep. He lay awake, grappling with the ethical dilemma before him. He had entered politics to make a difference, to fight for those who couldn't fight for themselves. But he was quickly learning that the path to change was fraught with challenges and compromises.

The next day, David scheduled a meeting with James Whitaker. They met in a private room at an upscale restaurant, the atmosphere tense.

"James, we need to talk about the land development deal," David said, his tone firm.

James raised an eyebrow. "I assume you understand the importance of this project. It's been in the works for years, and a lot of people stand to benefit from it."

"And a lot of people stand to lose their homes," David countered. "I can't support it as it stands. We need to find a way to ensure that those families are protected."

James leaned back in his chair, studying David. "You're making this difficult, David. The Power Brokers have invested a lot in your campaign. We expect you to cooperate."

David met his gaze, unwavering. "I understand your position, James. But my responsibility is to the people of this city. I'm willing to work with you to find a compromise, but I won't sacrifice my principles."

There was a long silence as the two men sized each other up. Finally, James nodded slowly. "Alright, David. We'll look into alternatives. But remember, you're playing a dangerous game. Make sure you don't bite the hand that feeds you."

As David left the meeting, he felt a mix of relief and apprehension. He had stood his ground, but he knew that his relationship with the Power Brokers was becoming increasingly strained. He had to be careful, but he also had to stay true to his mission.

The campaign continued to gain momentum. David's message of reform and integrity resonated with voters, and his popularity soared. He attended town hall meetings, engaged in spirited debates, and listened to the concerns of everyday citizens. He made a point to visit the neighborhoods most affected by the proposed land development, speaking directly with the families who faced displacement.

These interactions reinforced David's resolve. He saw the fear and uncertainty in their eyes, and he knew that he couldn't let them down. He worked tirelessly to find a solution that would satisfy the Power Brokers while protecting the vulnerable.

One evening, as David was preparing for a major campaign rally, he received an unexpected visitor. Emily Reyes, a respected journalist known for her hard-hitting investigative work, had requested an interview. David agreed, knowing that gaining the support of the media was crucial.

They sat down in his office, and Emily wasted no time getting to the point. "David, your campaign has been gaining a lot of traction. But with that comes scrutiny. There are rumors about your connections to the Power Brokers. Can you address that?"

David took a deep breath, choosing his words carefully. "Emily, I entered this race to bring about real change. Yes, I've received support from influential groups, including the Power Brokers. But I want to make it clear that my allegiance is to the people of this city. I've faced pressure to make compromises, but I remain committed to my principles."

Emily nodded, her expression thoughtful. "And what about the land development deal? There are concerns that it will displace low-income families."

David's jaw tightened. "I share those concerns. That's why I've been working to find a solution that protects those families. I've had difficult conversations with my backers, and I'm pushing for a compromise that minimizes harm."

Emily's eyes narrowed slightly. "Do you think you can win this battle, David? The Power Brokers are powerful and they don't take kindly to defiance."

David met her gaze, determination in his eyes. "I believe that with the support of the people, we can win. Change is never easy, but it's worth fighting for."

The interview aired the next day, and it had a profound impact. David's honesty and resolve resonated with viewers, and his support grew even stronger. The Power Brokers, aware of the shifting tides, became more cautious in their demands, recognizing that David's popularity made him a force to be reckoned with.

As the election drew closer, David's campaign reached a fever pitch. The final weeks were a blur of rallies, debates, and endless meetings. David barely slept, fueled by adrenaline and a relentless drive to succeed. His team worked around the clock, their dedication unwavering.

On the eve of the election, David stood before a massive crowd at his final rally. The energy was electric, and he could feel the weight of their hopes and dreams resting on his shoulders. As he took the stage, the cheers were deafening.

"Thank you," David said, his voice filled with emotion. "This campaign has been an incredible journey, and I am humbled by your support. Together, we've shown that change is possible. We've proven that integrity and justice can prevail. Tomorrow, we have a chance to make history. Let's take that chance and create a future we can all be proud of."

The crowd erupted into applause, and David felt a surge of hope and determination. This was it – the culmination of months of hard work and sacrifice. He had faced countless challenges, but he had stayed true to his vision.

Election day was a whirlwind. David and his team monitored the results from their headquarters, the tension palpable. As the hours ticked by, it became clear that the race was incredibly close. Every vote counted, and every minute felt like an eternity.

Finally, late into the night, the results were announced. David Collins had won the mayoral election by a narrow margin. The room erupted in cheers and tears of joy. David stood at the center, overwhelmed by the magnitude of the moment.

He had done it. He had become the new mayor, and now the real work began. David knew that his victory was just the beginning. He faced a daunting task – to reform a corrupt political system and create a government that truly served its people. But he was ready. He had the support of the city, and he was determined to make a difference.

As he stood before the jubilant crowd, David felt a deep sense of gratitude and responsibility. He had been given a chance to lead, and he would not squander it. The road ahead would be challenging, but he was ready to face it head-on.

With the city behind him and his vision clear, David Collins, the new candidate who had become the new mayor, embarked on a journey to transform his city and fulfill the promise of a better future for all.

Chapter 2: The Hidden Agenda

David Collins sat behind the grand oak desk in his new office, the expansive windows behind him offering a panoramic view of the city's skyline. The sight, once a symbol of ambition and hope, now felt like a heavy burden. He had been in office for only a few weeks, but the pressures and responsibilities of his position weighed heavily on his shoulders.

The early days had been filled with a flurry of activity – meeting with key advisors, outlining his initial policy proposals, and establishing his administration's priorities. The excitement of his victory had not yet worn off, and his team was eager to hit the ground running. But amidst the whirlwind of activity, David couldn't shake an uneasy feeling that had been growing in the back of his mind.

It started with subtle hints and whispers, the kind that were easy to dismiss as paranoia or overactive imagination. But as the days passed, these whispers grew louder and more persistent. David began to notice a pattern – the Power Brokers, the shadowy group that had supported his campaign, were exerting increasing influence over his decisions. Their suggestions, once helpful and aligned with his vision, now seemed to carry an undertone of coercion.

David prided himself on being an astute observer, a skill honed during his years as a public defender and advocate. He paid close attention to the interactions between his staff and the representatives of the Power Brokers. Meetings that were supposed to be routine began to feel more like orchestrations, with outcomes seemingly predetermined by unseen forces.

One evening, David sat in his office long after the staff had gone home. The city lights twinkled outside, casting a soft glow over the room. He leaned back in his chair, reflecting on the events of the past few weeks. Something was not right, and he needed to get to the bottom of it.

His thoughts were interrupted by a knock on the door. Rachel, his campaign manager and now his chief of staff, entered the room. She looked concerned, and David could tell that she had something important to discuss.

"David, we need to talk," she said, closing the door behind her.

"What's on your mind, Rachel?" David asked, gesturing for her to take a seat.

Rachel sat down, her expression serious. "I've been going over some of the recent policy proposals and meeting notes. There's a pattern emerging, and it's troubling. The Power Brokers are pushing for policies that seem to benefit a select few at the expense of the general public."

David nodded, grateful for Rachel's insight. "I've noticed the same thing. Their influence is becoming more pronounced, and it's starting to undermine our agenda."

Rachel leaned forward, her voice low and urgent. "We need to be careful, David. The Power Brokers have invested a lot in your campaign, and they expect a return on their investment. But we can't let them dictate our policies. We have to find a way to push back without alienating them completely."

David sighed, running a hand through his hair. "I know, Rachel. It's a delicate balance. But we can't compromise our principles. We need to find out exactly what their agenda is and how we can counter it."

Rachel nodded in agreement. "I'll start looking into their connections and influence. We need to gather as much information as we can. In the meantime, we should proceed cautiously with any proposals that come from their camp."

Over the next few days, David and Rachel worked discreetly to uncover the extent of the Power Brokers' influence. They pored over documents, scrutinized meeting minutes, and spoke with trusted advisors who shared their concerns. The picture that emerged was both complex and disturbing.

The Power Brokers had their hands in numerous sectors – real estate, finance, healthcare, and more. Their influence extended beyond city politics, reaching into state and even national levels. They were masters of manipulation, using their wealth and connections to shape policies and control outcomes. And now, they were leveraging David's popularity and integrity to further their own interests.

David felt a growing sense of betrayal. He had entered politics to fight corruption and serve the people, not to become a pawn in a larger game.

But the Power Brokers had seen his potential and had backed him with the expectation that he would be their puppet.

One evening, as David sat in his office, he received a call from James Whitaker, the prominent figure among the Power Brokers. James had always been cordial, but there was an edge to his tone that made David uneasy.

"David, we need to discuss the upcoming zoning laws," James said, getting straight to the point. "There's a proposal on the table that we strongly support. It will pave the way for significant development in the city."

David knew exactly which proposal James was referring to. It was a controversial plan that would benefit a handful of developers while displacing numerous low-income families. David had already voiced his concerns about it.

"James, I've reviewed the proposal, and I have serious reservations," David replied, keeping his tone measured. "It doesn't align with our commitment to protecting vulnerable communities."

There was a brief pause before James spoke again, his voice colder. "David, we've supported you because we believe in your potential. But you need to understand that this is a two-way street. Our support comes with certain expectations."

David felt a surge of anger but kept it in check. "I appreciate your support, James. But I was elected to serve the people, not to advance private interests. I won't support policies that harm the very communities we should be protecting."

James's response was swift and cutting. "Be careful, David. Remember who helped you get to where you are. We expect results."

The call ended abruptly, leaving David fuming. He knew he had to act swiftly and decisively. The Power Brokers were clearly prepared to exert pressure, and he needed to be ready to counter their influence.

The next morning, David called an emergency meeting with his inner circle. Rachel, Tom, and a few other trusted advisors gathered in his office, the tension palpable.

"We have a serious problem," David began, outlining his conversation with James and the broader implications of the Power Brokers' influence. "We need to take a stand, but we also need to be strategic. We can't afford to lose their support entirely, but we can't let them dictate our policies."

Tom, his chief strategist, spoke up. "We need to rally public support. If we can demonstrate that these proposals are against the public's interest, we can build a case to counter their influence. We need to be transparent and communicate our concerns directly to the people."

Rachel agreed. "We also need to start building alliances with other influential figures and organizations who share our vision. If we can create a coalition of support, we can mitigate the Power Brokers' influence."

David nodded, appreciating their input. "Let's start by organizing town hall meetings and public forums. We'll present the facts and let the people decide. We also need to reach out to community leaders and advocacy groups. This is a fight for the soul of our city, and we need all the support we can get."

Over the next few weeks, David and his team launched a grassroots campaign to counter the Power Brokers' influence. They held town hall meetings, engaged with the media, and built alliances with community organizations. David's message was clear – he was committed to serving the people and fighting against corruption, even if it meant going up against powerful interests.

The response from the public was overwhelmingly positive. People appreciated David's honesty and his willingness to stand up for what was right. His popularity soared, and the Power Brokers found themselves facing an unexpected challenge.

One evening, David received an anonymous tip. It was a set of documents that detailed the Power Brokers' involvement in various shady dealings, including bribery, coercion, and illegal lobbying. The documents were damning, providing concrete evidence of their manipulation and corruption.

David knew that releasing these documents would be a risky move. The Power Brokers were powerful and vindictive, and they would not take kindly to being exposed. But he also knew that he had a responsibility to the people who had elected him.

After discussing the documents with his team, David decided to go public. They organized a press conference, and David stood before the cameras, holding the evidence that would expose the Power Brokers for what they truly were.

"Today, I stand before you not just as your mayor, but as a servant of the people," David began, his voice steady and resolute. "I have uncovered evidence of widespread corruption and manipulation by a group of individuals who have sought to control our city's policies for their own benefit. These documents reveal their illegal activities and their attempts to undermine our democracy."

He held up the documents, letting the cameras capture the incriminating evidence. "I am committed to transparency and justice. I will not allow our city to be held hostage by those who seek to exploit it for personal gain. We will pursue legal action against these individuals, and we will work tirelessly to restore integrity to our political system."

The press conference sent shockwaves through the city. The media coverage was extensive, and public outrage grew as the details of the Power Brokers' activities came to light. The pressure mounted on the authorities to take action, and investigations were launched into the group's dealings.

James Whitaker and his associates were quick to respond, using their resources to mount a defense and discredit David's claims. They launched a counter-campaign, painting David as a reckless politician who was willing to undermine the city's stability for his own gain. The battle for public opinion was fierce, with both sides engaging in a war of words and tactics.

Despite the onslaught, David remained steadfast. He continued to engage with the public, attending town hall meetings and speaking directly to the people. He knew that his strength lay in his connection with the citizens, and he leveraged that connection to rally support.

The investigations into the Power Brokers' activities progressed, and the evidence against them continued to mount. Public sentiment shifted further in David's favor as more details of the corruption were revealed. It became clear that David's actions were motivated by a genuine desire to serve the people, rather than personal gain.

In the midst of the turmoil, David received unexpected support from a surprising source. Emily Reyes, the journalist who had interviewed him earlier, had been conducting her own investigation into the Power Brokers. She approached David with additional evidence that corroborated his claims and provided further insight into the group's machinations.

"David, I believe in what you're doing," Emily said, handing him a folder filled with documents. "I've been digging into the Power Brokers for months, and what I've found is even more damning than what you have. Together, we can bring them down."

David was grateful for Emily's support. With her help, they were able to build an even stronger case against the Power Brokers. The combined weight of the evidence and the growing public pressure made it increasingly difficult for the authorities to ignore.

As the legal proceedings moved forward, David's administration focused on implementing the reforms he had promised during his campaign. They prioritized transparency, accountability, and policies that benefited the broader community rather than a select few. The fight against the Power Brokers had galvanized his team and reinforced their commitment to creating a better city.

One evening, as David sat in his office reflecting on the journey so far, Rachel walked in with a smile on her face. "David, I have good news. The first phase of the investigation is complete, and several key members of the Power Brokers have been indicted. The tide is turning."

David felt a sense of relief and accomplishment. The battle was far from over, but they had made significant progress. "That's fantastic news, Rachel. We've come a long way, and we're making a real difference."

Rachel nodded, her eyes filled with determination. "We have, and we will continue to fight. This city deserves a government that truly serves its people. And we're going to make sure that happens."

David smiled, feeling a renewed sense of purpose. The journey had been challenging, and there were undoubtedly more obstacles ahead. But he knew that they were on the right path. The hidden agenda of the Power Brokers had been exposed, and their grip on the city's politics was weakening.

As David looked out over the city once more, he felt a sense of hope. The skyline, once a symbol of ambition and burden, now represented the potential for genuine change. He had made a promise to the people, and he was determined to see it through.

The hidden agenda had been uncovered, and the fight for integrity and justice was well underway. David Collins, with the support of his team and the people, was ready to lead the charge into a new era of transparency and accountability. The journey was far from over, but the path was clear, and the future looked brighter than ever before.

Chapter 3: Allies and Enemies

David Collins stood at the podium of a packed town hall meeting, the room buzzing with anticipation. It had been a month since he had exposed the Power Brokers' corrupt activities, and the fallout had been immense. Public opinion had swung firmly in his favor, and he was now focused on building alliances with other politicians and activists who shared his vision for reform. However, as his influence grew, so did the number of powerful enemies who felt threatened by his rise and the potential disruption to the status quo.

"Thank you all for being here today," David began, his voice clear and resonant. "Our city is at a crossroads. We have an opportunity to create a government that truly serves its people, but we cannot do it alone. We need to come together, to form alliances, and to support each other in this fight for justice and integrity."

The crowd erupted into applause, and David took a moment to scan the room. He recognized many familiar faces – community leaders, activists, and fellow politicians who had been vocal supporters of his campaign. But there were also new faces, people who had been inspired by his actions and were eager to join the movement.

After the meeting, David mingled with the attendees, shaking hands and engaging in earnest conversations. He was particularly keen to speak with several influential figures who had shown interest in collaborating with his administration.

One of these figures was Sarah Thompson, a respected state senator known for her progressive policies and commitment to social justice. Sarah had been a vocal critic of the Power Brokers and had expressed her support for David's efforts to expose their corruption.

"Senator Thompson, it's a pleasure to see you here," David said, extending his hand.

"Please, call me Sarah," she replied, shaking his hand warmly. "I'm impressed with what you've accomplished, David. Exposing the Power Brokers took real courage."

"Thank you, Sarah. Your support means a lot," David said sincerely. "I believe we share many of the same goals. I'd love to discuss how we can work together to push for meaningful reforms."

Sarah nodded. "Absolutely. Let's set up a meeting to discuss our plans in more detail. There are several initiatives I've been working on that I think could align well with your agenda."

As David continued to network, he also connected with Carlos Mendoza, a prominent activist and community organizer. Carlos had been instrumental in mobilizing grassroots support for David's campaign and was a fierce advocate for economic and social justice.

"Carlos, it's great to see you," David said, embracing his friend.

"David, you did it! You really shook things up," Carlos said, a wide grin on his face. "The community is behind you 100%. We need to keep this momentum going."

"I couldn't have done it without you and your team," David replied. "Your support was crucial. Let's talk about how we can continue to work together to address the issues that matter most to our communities."

Throughout the evening, David forged several key alliances with politicians, activists, and community leaders. These partnerships were essential to advancing his agenda and ensuring that the reforms he sought to implement had broad support. However, he was acutely aware that his rising influence also posed a threat to those who benefited from the existing power structures.

As David's administration moved forward with its reform agenda, resistance from powerful enemies began to mount. These adversaries included business leaders, political figures, and even some members of the media who had ties to the Power Brokers. They saw David's efforts as a direct challenge to their interests and were determined to undermine his administration.

One of the most formidable of these enemies was Richard Hawthorne, a wealthy industrialist with extensive political connections. Hawthorne had long been a beneficiary of the Power Brokers' influence and saw David's rise as a threat to his business empire.

David first became aware of Hawthorne's animosity during a heated city council meeting. The council was debating a proposal to increase environmental regulations on local industries, a measure that David strongly supported. Hawthorne, whose factories were among the largest polluters in the city, vehemently opposed the proposal.

"Mr. Mayor, these regulations are nothing more than a job-killing bureaucratic overreach," Hawthorne declared, his voice dripping with disdain. "If you push this through, you'll be putting thousands of hardworking people out of work."

David remained calm, though he could feel the tension in the room. "Mr. Hawthorne, these regulations are necessary to protect the health and well-being of our citizens. We cannot allow businesses to pollute our environment without consequence. I believe we can find a balance that supports both economic growth and environmental sustainability."

Hawthorne scoffed. "Balance? Your so-called reforms are driving businesses out of the city. You're destroying the very foundation of our economy."

The debate continued, but it was clear that Hawthorne was intent on opposing David at every turn. Despite the resistance, the city council ultimately passed the environmental regulations, marking a significant victory for David's administration. However, it also solidified Hawthorne's determination to bring David down.

As the weeks passed, Hawthorne and his allies launched a coordinated campaign to discredit David and his administration. They used their influence in the media to spread negative stories, accusing David of being anti-business and out of touch with the needs of the working class. The attacks were relentless, and David knew that he needed to respond effectively to counter the narrative.

David's inner circle, including Rachel and Tom, worked tirelessly to craft a strategy to combat the negative publicity. They focused on highlighting the positive impact of David's policies, showcasing success stories from the communities that had benefited from the reforms. They also organized public forums where David could engage directly with citizens and address their concerns.

One evening, as David prepared for a televised interview, Rachel pulled him aside. "David, this interview is crucial. We need to counter the negative narrative and reinforce your message of integrity and reform. Be honest, be relatable, and don't let them rattle you."

David nodded, appreciating Rachel's unwavering support. "I know. We've come too far to let them derail us now."

The interview was conducted by a seasoned journalist known for her tough questions. David was prepared, but he knew that he needed to be on his toes.

"Mayor Collins, there's been a lot of criticism about your administration's policies, particularly from the business community. How do you respond to claims that your reforms are hurting the local economy?" the journalist asked.

David took a deep breath, his expression resolute. "I understand the concerns, and I believe in the importance of a strong economy. But we cannot sacrifice the health and well-being of our citizens for short-term economic gains. Our policies are designed to create a sustainable future where businesses can thrive without harming the environment or exploiting workers. It's about finding a balance that benefits everyone."

The journalist pressed on. "What about the accusations that you're driving businesses out of the city and putting people out of work?"

David shook his head. "Those accusations are unfounded. In fact, we've seen new businesses opening and creating jobs as a result of our policies. We're investing in renewable energy, sustainable practices, and education to build a resilient economy. The challenges we face are significant, but I believe we're on the right path."

The interview continued, and David remained composed, addressing each question with clarity and conviction. By the end, he felt a sense of accomplishment, knowing that he had effectively communicated his vision and countered the negative narrative.

Despite the ongoing attacks from his enemies, David's alliances with other politicians and activists grew stronger. Sarah Thompson, Carlos Mendoza, and other key allies played crucial roles in advancing the reform agenda. Together, they pushed for policies that addressed systemic issues such as affordable housing, healthcare access, and criminal justice reform.

One of the most significant victories came with the passage of a comprehensive affordable housing initiative. The initiative aimed to increase the availability of affordable housing units, provide rental assistance to low-income families, and implement measures to prevent displacement due to gentrification. The legislation was a result of extensive collaboration between David's administration, community organizations, and supportive legislators.

At the signing ceremony, David stood alongside Sarah, Carlos, and other key allies. The room was filled with community members who had fought tirelessly for the initiative.

"Today is a testament to what we can achieve when we work together," David said, his voice filled with emotion. "This initiative will provide much-needed relief to countless families and ensure that everyone in our city has a place to call home. It's a step towards a more just and equitable society."

The applause was deafening, and David felt a deep sense of fulfillment. The road had been challenging, but moments like this reaffirmed his commitment to the cause.

However, the victories were not without their challenges. The powerful enemies who felt threatened by David's rise continued to plot against him. They sought to exploit any missteps and sow division within his administration. David knew that he had to remain vigilant and resilient in the face of these adversaries.

One evening, as David reviewed policy proposals in his office, Rachel walked in with a concerned expression. "David, we have a situation. We've received information that Richard Hawthorne is planning a major smear campaign. He's digging into your past, looking for anything he can use against you."

David sighed, feeling the weight of the ongoing battle. "I knew this was coming. We'll need to be prepared. Make sure our legal team is ready to counter any false claims, and let's double down on our outreach to the community. We need to keep our supporters informed and engaged."

Rachel nodded. "We'll get through this, David. You've faced bigger challenges before."

The smear campaign began in earnest, with Hawthorne's allies spreading rumors and innuendo about David's past. They painted him as a hypocrite, accusing him of engaging in the same corrupt practices he had vowed to fight. The attacks were personal and vicious, designed to undermine his credibility and erode public trust.

David's team worked tirelessly to counter the attacks, providing evidence to refute the false claims and highlighting his accomplishments and integrity. They also organized a series of public events where David could address the accusations directly and reaffirm his commitment to transparency and reform.

At one such event, held in a community center, David stood before a packed audience. The atmosphere was tense, and he could see the concern and doubt in the eyes of some of the attendees.

"Thank you all for being here," David began, his voice steady but filled with emotion. "I know that many of you have heard the accusations being leveled against me. Let me be clear – these claims are false, and they are being spread by those who seek to undermine our movement for their own gain."

He paused, looking around the room, making eye contact with as many people as he could. "I entered public service to fight for justice and integrity, and I remain committed to that cause. My record speaks for itself. We've made significant progress in addressing corruption, protecting the environment, and supporting our communities. But the fight is far from over."

David took a deep breath, feeling the weight of the moment. "I ask for your continued support and trust. Together, we can overcome these challenges and create a city that works for everyone. I promise to remain transparent and accountable, and I will not be swayed by those who seek to protect their own interests at the expense of the public good."

The room erupted into applause, and David felt a renewed sense of determination. The support of the community was his greatest strength, and he knew that he could rely on them to stand by him in the face of adversity.

As the months passed, the battles with his enemies continued, but so did the progress. David's alliances with other politicians and activists proved to be invaluable. Together, they achieved significant victories in areas such as healthcare reform, education funding, and criminal justice reform.

One of the most notable achievements was the passage of a comprehensive healthcare reform bill. The legislation expanded access to affordable healthcare, increased funding for mental health services, and implemented measures to address health disparities in underserved communities. The bill was a result of extensive collaboration between David's administration, healthcare advocates, and supportive legislators.

At the signing ceremony, David stood alongside Sarah, Carlos, and other key allies. The room was filled with healthcare workers, patients, and community members who had fought tirelessly for the reform.

"Today is a victory for our entire city," David said, his voice filled with pride. "This healthcare reform will ensure that everyone, regardless of their background or income, has access to the care they need. It's a testament to what we can achieve when we come together to fight for justice and equity."

The applause was thunderous, and David felt a deep sense of fulfillment. The journey had been challenging, but moments like this reaffirmed his commitment to the cause.

Despite the ongoing attacks from his enemies, David's administration continued to make strides in advancing their reform agenda. The powerful enemies who felt threatened by his rise grew increasingly desperate, but David remained resolute in his mission.

One evening, as David sat in his office reflecting on the journey so far, Rachel walked in with a smile on her face. "David, I have good news. The investigation into the Power Brokers is progressing, and several key members have been indicted. The tide is turning."

David felt a sense of relief and accomplishment. The battle was far from over, but they had made significant progress. "That's fantastic news, Rachel. We've come a long way, and we're making a real difference."

Rachel nodded, her eyes filled with determination. "We have, and we will continue to fight. This city deserves a government that truly serves its people. And we're going to make sure that happens."

David smiled, feeling a renewed sense of purpose. The journey had been challenging, and there were undoubtedly more obstacles ahead. But he knew that they were on the right path. The alliances he had forged with other politicians and activists had strengthened their movement, and the support of the community remained unwavering.

As David looked out over the city once more, he felt a sense of hope. The skyline, once a symbol of ambition and burden, now represented the potential for genuine change. He had made a promise to the people, and he was determined to see it through.

The battles with his enemies were far from over, but David Collins was ready to face them head-on. With the support of his allies and the community, he would continue to fight for a city that truly served its people. The path was clear, and the future looked brighter than ever before.

Chapter 4: The Media War

The city buzzed with the energy of a new political era as Mayor David Collins continued his crusade against corruption and inequity. But as his popularity grew, so did the challenges he faced. The Power Brokers, a shadowy group of influential individuals who had initially supported his campaign, were now leveraging their control over the media to shape public opinion and discredit David's opponents. This new battleground, the media war, posed complex ethical dilemmas for David and his administration.

David's day began early with a flurry of activity in his office. His chief of staff, Rachel, and his communications director, Tom, were already poring over the morning's headlines. The front pages of the city's newspapers were filled with stories about his administration's initiatives and the ongoing investigations into the Power Brokers. But there were also negative pieces, clearly designed to undermine his efforts and cast doubt on his integrity.

"David, we need to talk about our media strategy," Rachel said, her tone urgent. "The Power Brokers are using their media connections to launch a full-scale attack on us. They're framing our policies as radical and irresponsible, and it's starting to influence public opinion."

David nodded, understanding the gravity of the situation. "I know, Rachel. But we can't stoop to their level. We need to find a way to counter their narrative without compromising our principles."

Tom chimed in, his expression serious. "We need to be proactive. We can't just react to their attacks. We need to get ahead of the story, control the narrative, and highlight the positive impact of our policies. We also need to build stronger relationships with journalists who are committed to objective reporting."

The team spent the next few hours strategizing. They decided to organize a series of press conferences, town hall meetings, and public forums where David could engage directly with the media and the public. They also planned to ramp up their social media presence, using it as a platform to share success stories and counter misinformation.

David knew that the media war would be a long and arduous battle, but he was determined to stay true to his values. He believed in transparency, accountability, and the power of honest communication. However, as the attacks intensified, he began to feel the strain of navigating the ethical complexities of the situation.

One evening, as David prepared for a live television interview, he received a call from an unexpected source. Emily Reyes, the investigative journalist who had helped expose the Power Brokers, had uncovered new information that could potentially shift the tide in David's favor.

"David, I have something you need to see," Emily said, her voice urgent. "I've obtained documents that show the extent of the Power Brokers' manipulation of the media. They have been paying off journalists, planting fake stories, and using intimidation tactics to control the narrative."

David's heart raced as he listened to Emily's revelations. "This is huge, Emily. If we can expose this, it could turn the tables on them. But we need to handle this carefully. We can't afford to make any mistakes."

"I agree," Emily replied. "I'll send you the documents, and we can coordinate on how to release the information. We need to ensure that it's airtight and that we have the support of credible media outlets."

David thanked Emily and immediately called an emergency meeting with his team. They reviewed the documents and began formulating a plan to expose the Power Brokers' media manipulation. They knew that timing and execution were critical.

The next morning, David held a press conference to address the city's media. The room was packed with journalists, cameras, and reporters, all eager to hear what he had to say.

"Good morning," David began, his voice steady and resolute. "Today, I stand before you to address a matter of great importance. Over the past few months, my administration has faced relentless attacks from powerful interests who seek to undermine our efforts to bring about meaningful change. These attacks have been orchestrated through a campaign of misinformation and manipulation, and I have evidence to prove it."

He held up the documents that Emily had provided. "These documents reveal the extent to which the Power Brokers have gone to control the media and shape public opinion. They have paid off journalists, planted fake stories, and used intimidation tactics to silence dissent. This is an assault on our democracy and the principles of free and independent journalism."

The room erupted in murmurs and whispers as the journalists processed the gravity of David's accusations. He continued, laying out the evidence in detail and calling for a thorough investigation into the Power Brokers' activities.

The press conference had a profound impact. The story dominated the headlines, and public outrage grew as more details emerged about the Power Brokers' manipulation of the media. The authorities launched an investigation, and several journalists and media executives were implicated in the scandal.

However, the media war was far from over. The Power Brokers, sensing the threat to their influence, doubled down on their efforts to discredit David and his administration. They used their remaining connections to spread false information and create doubt about the legitimacy of the documents.

David and his team worked tirelessly to counter these attacks. They continued to engage with the public, highlighting the positive impact of their policies and the importance of integrity in governance. They also focused on building alliances with journalists who were committed to objective and ethical reporting.

One of the key strategies was to humanize the stories behind their policies. David and his team organized community events where citizens who had benefited from their initiatives could share their experiences. These stories were powerful and resonated deeply with the public.

At one such event, held in a community center, David stood alongside a young mother named Maria, who had been able to secure affordable housing thanks to the administration's initiatives.

"Maria, thank you for being here," David said, his voice warm and empathetic. "Can you share with us how the affordable housing initiative has impacted your life?"

Maria nodded, her eyes filled with gratitude. "Before this initiative, I was struggling to find a safe and affordable place for my children and me. We were constantly moving from one place to another, never knowing if we'd have a roof over our heads. But thanks to this program, we now have a stable home. My children are doing better in school, and I can focus on providing for them without the constant worry of being displaced."

The audience erupted into applause, and David felt a surge of pride. Stories like Maria's were a testament to the positive impact of their policies, and they helped to counter the negative narratives being pushed by the Power Brokers.

Despite their efforts, the ethical dilemmas of the media war continued to weigh heavily on David. He knew that the Power Brokers were willing to use any means necessary to achieve their goals, and he struggled with the question of how far he should go to counter their tactics without compromising his own principles.

One evening, as David sat in his office reflecting on the ongoing battle, Rachel walked in with a concerned expression. "David, we need to talk," she said, closing the door behind her.

"What's on your mind, Rachel?" David asked, sensing the gravity of the conversation.

Rachel took a deep breath. "We've received intel that the Power Brokers are planning to release a fabricated story about you. They're going to accuse you of financial misconduct, and they've even created fake documents to support their claims. This is going to be a major hit, and we need to be prepared."

David felt a knot in his stomach. "We need to counter this immediately. We can't let them get away with it."

Rachel nodded. "I agree. But we also need to be careful. If we respond too aggressively, it could backfire and make us look defensive. We need to find a way to expose their lies without stooping to their level."

David sighed, feeling the weight of the ethical complexities. "You're right, Rachel. We need to maintain our integrity. Let's gather our legal team and prepare a response. We'll also reach out to our allies in the media to ensure that the truth gets out."

The next few days were a whirlwind of activity as David's team prepared to counter the impending attack. They gathered evidence to refute the fabricated claims and coordinated with supportive journalists to ensure that the truth would be reported.

When the Power Brokers released their fabricated story, David was ready. He held a press conference to address the accusations head-on, presenting the evidence that exposed the falsehoods and reaffirming his commitment to transparency and accountability.

"These accusations are baseless and malicious," David declared, his voice resolute. "The documents presented by my opponents are fabrications, designed to undermine our efforts to bring about meaningful change. We have provided evidence to refute these claims, and we will continue to stand strong in the face of these attacks."

The public response was overwhelmingly supportive. The Power Brokers' attempt to discredit David had backfired, and their credibility was further eroded. The investigation into their activities continued, and more revelations about their manipulation of the media came to light.

Despite the victories, the media war took a toll on David and his team. The constant barrage of attacks and the need to constantly defend their integrity were exhausting. David often found himself questioning whether he could continue to fight this battle without compromising his values.

One evening, as David sat in his office feeling the weight of the ongoing struggle, he received a visit from Carlos Mendoza, the activist and community organizer who had been a steadfast ally.

"David, I know this has been tough," Carlos said, his voice filled with empathy. "But you need to remember why you started this journey. You're fighting for the people, for justice, and for a better future. Don't let the Power Brokers' tactics make you lose sight of that."

David nodded, grateful for Carlos's support. "I know, Carlos. It's just hard sometimes. The constant attacks, the ethical dilemmas... it's a lot to handle."

Carlos placed a hand on David's shoulder. "You're not alone in this fight. You have a team of dedicated people who believe in you and the work you're doing. And you have the support of the community. We'll get through this together."

David felt a renewed sense of determination. The media war was a challenging and complex battleground, but he was not alone. With the support of his team, his allies, and the community, he would continue to fight for justice and integrity.

As the months passed, the media war continued, but David's administration remained resilient. They achieved significant victories, including the passage of new legislation to increase transparency and accountability in government. These reforms were a direct response to the corruption exposed by the Power Brokers' activities, and they were a testament to David's commitment to creating a more just and equitable city.

One of the most notable achievements was the creation of an independent oversight commission to monitor government activities and ensure transparency. The commission was composed of respected community leaders, legal experts, and journalists, and it had the authority to investigate allegations of corruption and misconduct.

At the inauguration ceremony for the oversight commission, David stood alongside Sarah Thompson, Carlos Mendoza, and other key allies. The room was filled with community members, activists, and journalists who had fought tirelessly for this reform.

"Today marks a significant step forward in our fight for justice and integrity," David said, his voice filled with pride. "This oversight commission will ensure that our government remains accountable to the people it serves. It's a testament to what we can achieve when we come together to fight for what's right."

The applause was thunderous, and David felt a deep sense of fulfillment. The journey had been challenging, but moments like this reaffirmed his commitment to the cause.

Despite the ongoing attacks from the Power Brokers, David's administration continued to make strides in advancing their reform agenda. The media war was far from over, but David remained resolute in his mission. He knew that the fight for a more just and equitable city was a long and arduous journey, but he was determined to see it through.

One evening, as David sat in his office reflecting on the journey so far, Rachel walked in with a smile on her face. "David, I have good news. The investigation into the Power Brokers is progressing, and several key members have been indicted. The tide is turning."

David felt a sense of relief and accomplishment. The battle was far from over, but they had made significant progress. "That's fantastic news, Rachel. We've come a long way, and we're making a real difference."

Rachel nodded, her eyes filled with determination. "We have, and we will continue to fight. This city deserves a government that truly serves its people. And we're going to make sure that happens."

David smiled, feeling a renewed sense of purpose. The journey had been challenging, and there were undoubtedly more obstacles ahead. But he knew that they were on the right path. The media war was a complex and difficult battleground, but with the support of his team and the community, he would continue to fight for justice and integrity.

As David looked out over the city once more, he felt a sense of hope. The skyline, once a symbol of ambition and burden, now represented the potential for genuine change. He had made a promise to the people, and he was determined to see it through.

The media war had tested his resolve and his principles, but David Collins was ready to face the challenges ahead. With the support of his allies and the community, he would continue to fight for a city that truly served its people. The path was clear, and the future looked brighter than ever before.

Chapter 5: Secrets and Lies

The morning sunlight filtered through the windows of David Collins's office, casting a warm glow on the stacks of documents and folders that covered his desk. The city outside was bustling with life, but inside the mayor's office, the atmosphere was tense and focused. David's recent victories against the Power Brokers had earned him both admiration and increased scrutiny. Yet, as he delved deeper into the machinations of this shadowy group, he uncovered dark secrets that posed a new and formidable challenge.

David sat back in his chair, rubbing his temples as he reviewed the latest set of documents provided by Emily Reyes, the investigative journalist who had been instrumental in exposing the Power Brokers' media manipulation. These documents detailed a web of illegal activities and past political scandals involving some of the most influential members of the Power Brokers. The revelations were explosive, and the implications were far-reaching.

Rachel, his chief of staff, entered the office carrying a cup of coffee. She placed it on David's desk and looked at him with concern. "David, you look exhausted. You need to take a break."

David sighed, taking a sip of the coffee. "I know, Rachel. But we can't afford to let up now. The more we uncover about the Power Brokers, the more dangerous they seem. These latest documents... they reveal a level of corruption and criminal activity that goes beyond anything we imagined."

Rachel nodded, her expression serious. "I've read through them too. This is heavy stuff. We're talking about bribery, extortion, and even connections to organized crime. If we expose this, it could bring down some very powerful people."

David leaned forward, his gaze intense. "And that's exactly what they fear. But we have to be careful. If we move too quickly or without enough evidence, they'll find a way to discredit us. We need a solid plan to ensure that the truth comes out and that justice is served."

Rachel sat down across from him, her eyes filled with determination. "I agree. We need to gather more evidence and build a case that is airtight. We also need to think about the potential fallout. Exposing these secrets will shake the political landscape to its core. Are we prepared for the consequences?"

David nodded, appreciating Rachel's pragmatism. "We have to be. The people deserve to know the truth, and we have a responsibility to ensure that those who abuse their power are held accountable. But we need to be strategic about how we do this."

Over the next few days, David and his team worked tirelessly to piece together the evidence. They reached out to trusted allies, including legal experts, journalists, and community leaders, to help verify the information and prepare for the inevitable backlash. The revelations were shocking: several high-ranking officials had been involved in a range of illegal activities, from accepting bribes to cover up scandals to engaging in shady business deals with organized crime figures.

As they delved deeper, they uncovered a particularly disturbing connection involving Richard Hawthorne, the wealthy industrialist who had been one of David's most vocal adversaries. The documents revealed that Hawthorne had not only used his influence to manipulate city policies but had also been involved in a series of financial crimes, including money laundering and tax evasion. Additionally, there were indications that he had used intimidation and violence to silence those who opposed him.

One evening, as David reviewed the evidence with his team, Emily Reyes arrived with a new batch of documents. "David, I've got more," she said, her voice urgent. "These files detail Hawthorne's involvement in a cover-up of a major environmental disaster caused by one of his factories. He paid off officials to bury the evidence and avoid prosecution."

David's jaw tightened as he read through the documents. The cover-up had resulted in severe health issues for the residents of a nearby community, many of whom had suffered from respiratory illnesses and other health problems due to the pollution.

"This is unbelievable," David said, his voice filled with anger. "Hawthorne has caused so much harm, and he's managed to escape justice for years. We have to expose this."

Emily nodded. "I agree, but we need to be careful. Hawthorne has powerful allies, and he's not going to go down without a fight. We need to make sure that we have all our bases covered and that we can withstand the inevitable attacks."

David and his team spent the next few weeks meticulously building their case. They gathered testimonies from whistleblowers, compiled financial records, and verified the authenticity of the documents. The evidence was overwhelming, but David knew that presenting it in the right way was crucial.

As they prepared to go public, David faced a moral dilemma. Exposing these secrets would undoubtedly bring about justice, but it would also unleash a political firestorm. Innocent people could get caught in the crossfire, and the city's stability could be jeopardized. David wrestled with the ethical implications of his actions, knowing that the consequences would be far-reaching.

One evening, as David sat in his office contemplating his next move, Sarah Thompson, the state senator and one of his closest allies, walked in. She had been a vocal supporter of his efforts to reform the city and had played a key role in advancing their legislative agenda.

"David, I've heard about the new evidence you've uncovered," Sarah said, her voice filled with concern. "This is big. But we need to think about the broader implications. Exposing this corruption is the right thing to do, but it will also cause a lot of turmoil. Are you prepared for that?"

David looked at her, his expression somber. "I am, Sarah. But it's not an easy decision. I've been thinking a lot about the potential fallout. The people have a right to know the truth, but we need to make sure that we handle this responsibly. We can't afford to let the city descend into chaos."

Sarah nodded. "I understand. But we also can't let fear hold us back. If we don't take action, these people will continue to abuse their power and hurt the community. We have to find a way to strike a balance – to expose the truth while minimizing the damage."

David appreciated Sarah's wisdom and support. "You're right, Sarah. We need to be strategic and measured in our approach. Let's gather our key allies and discuss how we can move forward."

David called an emergency meeting with his inner circle, including Rachel, Tom, Carlos Mendoza, Emily Reyes, and a few trusted advisors. They reviewed the evidence and discussed their strategy for going public. The plan was to hold a press conference where they would present the evidence and call for an independent investigation into the Power Brokers' activities.

"We need to ensure that the press conference is airtight," Tom said, his tone serious. "We can't afford any missteps. We need to present the evidence clearly and concisely, and we need to be prepared for the backlash. The Power Brokers will fight back with everything they have."

Emily nodded in agreement. "I'll coordinate with the journalists I trust to make sure that the story gets out accurately. We also need to be prepared for legal challenges. The Power Brokers will try to discredit us and bury the evidence."

Carlos spoke up, his voice filled with determination. "We need to mobilize the community. If the people are behind us, it will be much harder for the Power Brokers to silence us. We should organize rallies and town hall meetings to build support and keep the pressure on."

David felt a renewed sense of purpose as he listened to his team. They were ready to take on this monumental challenge, and he knew that they had the strength and determination to see it through.

The day of the press conference arrived, and the room was packed with journalists, community leaders, and supporters. The atmosphere was charged with anticipation and tension. David stood at the podium, flanked by his team and key allies.

"Good morning," David began, his voice steady but filled with emotion. "Today, I stand before you to share evidence of corruption and criminal activities that have plagued our city for far too long. The documents we are about to present reveal a web of illegal activities involving some of the most powerful individuals in our city, including members of the Power Brokers."

He held up the documents, letting the cameras capture the incriminating evidence. "These documents detail acts of bribery, extortion, financial crimes, and even connections to organized crime. They also reveal a cover-up of a major environmental disaster caused by one of Richard Hawthorne's factories, which has resulted in severe health issues for the residents of a nearby community."

The room erupted into murmurs and gasps as David laid out the evidence in detail. He called for an independent investigation and urged the authorities to take swift action to bring those responsible to justice.

The press conference had an immediate and profound impact. The story dominated the headlines, and public outrage grew as more details emerged about the Power Brokers' activities. The authorities launched an investigation, and several high-ranking officials were implicated in the scandal.

However, the Power Brokers did not go down without a fight. They used their remaining influence to launch a counterattack, spreading false information and attempting to discredit David and his team. The battle for public opinion was fierce, with both sides engaging in a war of words and tactics.

David and his team remained resolute, continuing to engage with the public and build support for their cause. They organized rallies, town hall meetings, and public forums where citizens could voice their concerns and demand accountability.

One evening, as David prepared for a town hall meeting, he received a visit from a whistleblower who had come forward with additional evidence. The whistleblower, a former aide to one of the implicated officials, provided crucial information that further corroborated the documents and revealed even more damning details about the Power Brokers' activities.

"Thank you for coming forward," David said, his voice filled with gratitude. "Your courage is greatly appreciated. This information will be invaluable in our fight for justice."

The whistleblower nodded, their expression serious. "I couldn't stay silent any longer. What they did was wrong, and the people deserve to know the truth."

David and his team incorporated the new evidence into their case, strengthening their position and increasing the pressure on the authorities to take action. The investigation progressed, and more revelations about the Power Brokers' corruption came to light.

Despite the ongoing attacks from their enemies, David's administration continued to make strides in advancing their reform agenda. They achieved significant victories, including the passage of new legislation to increase transparency and accountability in government. These reforms were a direct response to the corruption exposed by the Power Brokers' activities, and they were a testament to David's commitment to creating a more just and equitable city.

One of the most notable achievements was the establishment of a special task force to investigate and prosecute cases of corruption and financial crimes. The task force was composed of experienced prosecutors, investigators, and legal experts, and it had the authority to pursue cases at all levels of government.

At the inauguration ceremony for the task force, David stood alongside Sarah Thompson, Carlos Mendoza, and other key allies. The room was filled with community members, activists, and journalists who had fought tirelessly for this reform.

"Today marks a significant step forward in our fight for justice and integrity," David said, his voice filled with pride. "This task force will ensure that those who abuse their power are held accountable and that our government remains transparent and accountable to the people it serves. It's a testament to what we can achieve when we come together to fight for what's right."

The applause was thunderous, and David felt a deep sense of fulfillment. The journey had been challenging, but moments like this reaffirmed his commitment to the cause.

Despite the ongoing attacks from the Power Brokers, David's administration continued to make strides in advancing their reform agenda. The media war was far from over, but David remained resolute in his mission. He knew that the fight for a more just and equitable city was a long and arduous journey, but he was determined to see it through.

One evening, as David sat in his office reflecting on the journey so far, Rachel walked in with a smile on her face. "David, I have good news. The investigation into the Power Brokers is progressing, and several key members have been indicted. The tide is turning."

David felt a sense of relief and accomplishment. The battle was far from over, but they had made significant progress. "That's fantastic news, Rachel. We've come a long way, and we're making a real difference."

Rachel nodded, her eyes filled with determination. "We have, and we will continue to fight. This city deserves a government that truly serves its people. And we're going to make sure that happens."

David smiled, feeling a renewed sense of purpose. The journey had been challenging, and there were undoubtedly more obstacles ahead. But he knew that they were on the right path. The secrets and lies of the Power Brokers had been exposed, and their grip on the city's politics was weakening.

As David looked out over the city once more, he felt a sense of hope. The skyline, once a symbol of ambition and burden, now represented the potential for genuine change. He had made a promise to the people, and he was determined to see it through.

The battle against the Power Brokers had tested his resolve and his principles, but David Collins was ready to face the challenges ahead. With the support of his allies and the community, he would continue to fight for a city that truly served its people. The path was clear, and the future looked brighter than ever before.

Chapter 6: The Turning Point

David Collins stood on the balcony of his office, looking out over the city that had become both his battleground and his beacon of hope. The sun was setting, casting a warm, golden hue across the skyline. It should have been a moment of tranquility, but David's mind was anything but calm. The weight of the secrets he had uncovered and the ethical dilemmas he faced pressed heavily on his conscience.

The recent victories against the Power Brokers had been significant, but the cost was becoming increasingly apparent. The media war, the political battles, and the constant scrutiny were taking their toll. Yet, it was the moral compromises he had been forced to consider that troubled him the most. The Power Brokers had initially supported his campaign, believing that they could control him and use his popularity to further their own agenda. But David had always been driven by a desire to serve the people and uphold justice, and the corruption he had uncovered had shaken him to his core.

As he stood there, lost in thought, Rachel walked out onto the balcony, her expression filled with concern. "David, you okay? You've been out here for a while."

David turned to her, his face etched with worry. "I don't know, Rachel. I can't shake the feeling that we're only scratching the surface. The more we uncover, the deeper the corruption seems to go. And the more I realize that we've been playing their game all along."

Rachel nodded, understanding his turmoil. "I know it's tough, David. But we've made significant progress. The public is behind us, and we're starting to see real change. You can't lose sight of that."

David sighed, running a hand through his hair. "I know. But I can't ignore the fact that the Power Brokers are still out there, pulling strings and manipulating the system. And now that we have more evidence of their unethical practices, I feel like we need to confront them directly. It's the only way to put an end to this once and for all."

Rachel's eyes widened in surprise. "Confront them? David, that's risky. You know how powerful they are. If we go after them head-on, they'll fight back with everything they have."

David nodded, his expression resolute. "I know the risks, Rachel. But I can't in good conscience continue to fight this battle from the shadows. The people deserve to know the truth, and we need to hold the Power Brokers accountable for their actions."

Rachel sighed, her concern deepening. "If you do this, you'll be putting yourself and everyone around you in danger. We need to be prepared for the fallout."

David placed a reassuring hand on her shoulder. "I understand, Rachel. But I believe this is the right thing to do. We've come too far to back down now. We need to take a stand."

The decision to confront the Power Brokers set in motion a series of events that would define the future of David's administration and the city itself. Over the next few days, David and his team worked tirelessly to prepare for the confrontation. They gathered additional evidence, secured the support of key allies, and developed a comprehensive strategy to expose the Power Brokers' unethical practices.

One evening, as David reviewed the final preparations with his team, Sarah Thompson, the state senator and one of his closest allies, walked in. She had been a steadfast supporter of his efforts and had played a crucial role in advancing their legislative agenda.

"David, I heard about your decision to confront the Power Brokers," Sarah said, her tone serious. "I admire your courage, but I want to make sure you're prepared for what's coming. This isn't going to be easy."

David looked up from his papers, meeting her gaze. "I know, Sarah. But I believe it's the right thing to do. We need to hold them accountable and show the people that we're committed to justice."

Sarah nodded, her expression thoughtful. "I agree. But we need to be strategic. The Power Brokers have a lot of influence, and they'll use every tool at their disposal to protect themselves. We need to anticipate their moves and be ready to counter them."

David appreciated her wisdom. "You're right, Sarah. We need to be smart about this. Let's discuss our strategy and make sure we're covering all our bases."

The next morning, David called a press conference to announce his intention to confront the Power Brokers directly. The room was packed with journalists, community leaders, and supporters, all eager to hear what he had to say.

"Good morning," David began, his voice steady but filled with emotion. "Over the past few months, my administration has been working tirelessly to expose corruption and bring about meaningful change in our city. We've made significant progress, but our work is far from over. Today, I am here to announce that we have uncovered further evidence of unethical practices and illegal activities involving the Power Brokers, a group of influential individuals who have been manipulating our political system for their own gain."

He paused, letting the weight of his words sink in. "I have decided to confront the Power Brokers directly and hold them accountable for their actions. This is not a decision I have made lightly, but it is one that I believe is necessary for the future of our city. The people deserve to know the truth, and we need to ensure that those who abuse their power are brought to justice."

The room erupted into murmurs and gasps as David laid out the evidence in detail. He called for an independent investigation and urged the authorities to take swift action to address the corruption. The announcement sent shockwaves through the city, and the response was immediate and intense.

As expected, the Power Brokers did not take the confrontation lightly. They used their remaining influence to launch a counterattack, spreading false information and attempting to discredit David and his team. The battle for public opinion was fierce, with both sides engaging in a war of words and tactics.

David and his team remained resolute, continuing to engage with the public and build support for their cause. They organized rallies, town hall meetings, and public forums where citizens could voice their concerns and demand accountability.

One evening, as David prepared for a town hall meeting, he received a visit from Emily Reyes, the investigative journalist who had been instrumental in uncovering the Power Brokers' activities.

"David, I wanted to let you know that I've been digging deeper into the Power Brokers' connections," Emily said, her voice urgent. "I've found evidence that ties them to a series of financial crimes and political scandals that go back years. This could be the smoking gun we need to bring them down."

David's eyes widened in surprise. "That's incredible, Emily. This could change everything. But we need to handle this carefully. The Power Brokers will do everything they can to bury this evidence and discredit us."

Emily nodded. "I know. But we can't let them get away with it. We need to make sure that the truth comes out and that justice is served."

David felt a renewed sense of determination. The evidence Emily had uncovered was the key to exposing the full extent of the Power Brokers' corruption. They needed to act quickly and decisively to ensure that the truth was revealed.

The next few days were a whirlwind of activity as David and his team prepared to present the new evidence. They coordinated with their allies, briefed the media, and developed a comprehensive strategy to ensure that the information was disseminated accurately and effectively.

On the day of the press conference, the atmosphere was charged with anticipation and tension. The room was filled with journalists, community leaders, and supporters, all eager to hear what David had to say.

"Good morning," David began, his voice steady but filled with emotion. "Today, I stand before you to share new evidence that further exposes the corruption and unethical practices of the Power Brokers. This evidence reveals a series of financial crimes and political scandals that have been orchestrated by this group for years. We have a responsibility to ensure that those who abuse their power are held accountable and that justice is served."

He held up the documents, letting the cameras capture the incriminating evidence. "We are calling for an independent investigation to thoroughly examine these allegations and take appropriate action against those involved. The people deserve to know the truth, and we are committed to ensuring that justice is served."

The press conference had an immediate and profound impact. The story dominated the headlines, and public outrage grew as more details emerged about the Power Brokers' activities. The authorities launched an investigation, and several high-ranking officials were implicated in the scandal.

Despite the victories, the ethical dilemmas continued to weigh heavily on David. He knew that the confrontation with the Power Brokers would have far-reaching consequences, and he wrestled with the moral implications of his actions. He was determined to stay true to his principles, but the challenges ahead were daunting.

One evening, as David sat in his office reflecting on the journey so far, Carlos Mendoza, the activist and community organizer who had been a steadfast ally, walked in.

"David, I know this has been tough," Carlos said, his voice filled with empathy. "But you need to remember why you started this journey. You're fighting for the people, for justice, and for a better future. Don't let the Power Brokers' tactics make you lose sight of that."

David nodded, grateful for Carlos's support. "I know, Carlos. It's just hard sometimes. The constant attacks, the ethical dilemmas... it's a lot to handle."

Carlos placed a hand on David's shoulder. "You're not alone in this fight. You have a team of dedicated people who believe in you and the work you're doing. And you have the support of the community. We'll get through this together."

David felt a renewed sense of determination. The confrontation with the Power Brokers was a challenging and complex battleground, but he was not alone. With the support of his team, his allies, and the community, he would continue to fight for justice and integrity.

As the weeks passed, the investigation into the Power Brokers progressed, and more revelations about their corruption came to light.

The authorities took swift action, and several high-ranking officials were indicted. The city's political landscape began to shift, and there was a renewed sense of hope and optimism among the citizens.

One of the most significant victories came with the passage of new legislation to increase transparency and accountability in government. These reforms were a direct response to the corruption exposed by the Power Brokers' activities, and they were a testament to David's commitment to creating a more just and equitable city.

At the signing ceremony for the new legislation, David stood alongside Sarah Thompson, Carlos Mendoza, and other key allies. The room was filled with community members, activists, and journalists who had fought tirelessly for this reform.

"Today marks a significant step forward in our fight for justice and integrity," David said, his voice filled with pride. "This legislation will ensure that our government remains transparent and accountable to the people it serves. It's a testament to what we can achieve when we come together to fight for what's right."

The applause was thunderous, and David felt a deep sense of fulfillment. The journey had been challenging, but moments like this reaffirmed his commitment to the cause.

Despite the ongoing attacks from the Power Brokers, David's administration continued to make strides in advancing their reform agenda. The confrontation had tested his resolve and his principles, but he remained resolute in his mission. He knew that the fight for a more just and equitable city was a long and arduous journey, but he was determined to see it through.

One evening, as David sat in his office reflecting on the journey so far, Rachel walked in with a smile on her face. "David, I have good news. The investigation into the Power Brokers is progressing, and several key members have been indicted. The tide is turning."

David felt a sense of relief and accomplishment. The battle was far from over, but they had made significant progress. "That's fantastic news, Rachel. We've come a long way, and we're making a real difference."

Rachel nodded, her eyes filled with determination. "We have, and we will continue to fight. This city deserves a government that truly serves its people. And we're going to make sure that happens."

David smiled, feeling a renewed sense of purpose. The journey had been challenging, and there were undoubtedly more obstacles ahead. But he knew that they were on the right path. The confrontation with the Power Brokers had been a turning point, and their grip on the city's politics was weakening.

As David looked out over the city once more, he felt a sense of hope. The skyline, once a symbol of ambition and burden, now represented the potential for genuine change. He had made a promise to the people, and he was determined to see it through.

The battle against the Power Brokers had tested his resolve and his principles, but David Collins was ready to face the challenges ahead. With the support of his allies and the community, he would continue to fight for a city that truly served its people. The path was clear, and the future looked brighter than ever before.

Chapter 7: Betrayal

David Collins was riding high on the momentum of recent victories. His administration's reforms were gaining traction, the Power Brokers' grip on the city was weakening, and public support for his efforts was stronger than ever. But beneath the surface, a storm was brewing, one that would test his resolve and threaten everything he had worked so hard to achieve.

It started subtly, with small setbacks that seemed inconsequential at first. A critical piece of legislation was delayed, confidential information leaked to the press, and a key ally suddenly turned against him on an important vote. David dismissed these incidents as the usual challenges of political life, unaware that they were the first signs of a deeper betrayal.

One afternoon, as David reviewed the latest poll numbers with his chief of staff, Rachel, and his communications director, Tom, his phone buzzed with a text message from Emily Reyes, the investigative journalist who had become one of his most trusted allies.

"David, we need to talk. Urgent. Meet me at the usual spot."

David frowned, his gut tightening with a sense of foreboding. He excused himself from the meeting and headed to the coffee shop where he and Emily often met to discuss sensitive matters. Emily was already there, her expression grim as she sipped her coffee.

"Emily, what's going on?" David asked as he sat down across from her.

Emily glanced around to ensure they were not overheard, then leaned in. "David, I've been doing some digging, and I've uncovered something troubling. One of your closest allies is a double agent, working for your political enemies."

David felt as if the ground had shifted beneath him. "What? Who?"

Emily took a deep breath. "It's Carlos Mendoza."

David's mind reeled. Carlos, the passionate activist and community organizer who had been with him from the beginning, who had stood by his side through every battle. The idea that Carlos could betray him was unthinkable.

"Are you sure?" David asked, his voice barely above a whisper.

Emily nodded, her expression filled with regret. "I've got solid evidence. He's been feeding information to the Power Brokers and coordinating with them to undermine your efforts. The recent leaks and setbacks – they're all connected to him."

David sat back, feeling a mix of anger and disbelief. "Why would he do this? What could they have offered him?"

Emily shook her head. "I'm still trying to figure that out. But whatever the reason, we need to act quickly. If we don't address this betrayal, it could lead to a major political setback."

David nodded, his mind racing. "We need to confront him and gather more evidence. But we also need to be strategic. If we handle this wrong, it could blow up in our faces."

Emily agreed. "I'll continue investigating and see if I can uncover more details. In the meantime, you need to figure out how to address this internally without causing a panic."

David returned to his office, his thoughts consumed by the revelation. He called an emergency meeting with Rachel and Tom, careful to exclude Carlos.

"What's going on, David?" Rachel asked, sensing the tension.

David took a deep breath. "I've just learned that Carlos is a double agent, working for the Power Brokers. Emily has evidence that he's been feeding them information and coordinating with them to undermine us."

Rachel and Tom exchanged shocked glances. "Carlos? That can't be," Tom said. "He's been one of our strongest supporters."

David nodded. "I know. But the evidence is solid. We need to figure out how to handle this. If we move too quickly, it could cause a scandal. But if we don't act, it could lead to a major political setback."

Rachel sighed, her expression thoughtful. "We need to gather more evidence and build a case. If we can confront him with irrefutable proof, we can minimize the fallout. But we also need to be prepared for the public reaction."

Tom agreed. "We should also start identifying potential replacements for Carlos. If we have someone ready to step in, it will help stabilize the situation."

David nodded. "Let's get to work. We need to move quickly and carefully."

Over the next few days, David and his team worked tirelessly to gather more evidence against Carlos. Emily continued her investigation, uncovering more details about Carlos's betrayal. The evidence was damning: emails, phone records, and financial transactions that tied Carlos directly to the Power Brokers.

As they prepared to confront Carlos, David felt a mix of anger, sadness, and determination. The betrayal cut deep, but he knew that he needed to stay focused on the bigger picture. The future of their reforms and the city's well-being depended on their response.

The confrontation took place in David's office, with Rachel, Tom, and Emily present. Carlos walked in, his usual confident demeanor replaced by a look of confusion and apprehension.

"What's going on, David?" Carlos asked, glancing around the room.

David took a deep breath, meeting Carlos's gaze. "Carlos, we need to talk. We've uncovered evidence that you've been working with the Power Brokers, feeding them information and coordinating with them to undermine our efforts."

Carlos's eyes widened in shock. "What? That's ridiculous! I've been with you from the beginning, fighting for the same goals."

David held up a stack of documents. "The evidence says otherwise. Emails, phone records, financial transactions – they all point to your involvement. Why, Carlos? Why would you betray us?"

Carlos's face paled, and he looked down, unable to meet David's eyes. "It's not what you think, David. They approached me months ago, threatened me and my family. They said they'd ruin my life if I didn't cooperate."

David felt a surge of anger. "And you didn't think to come to us? To tell us what was happening?"

Carlos shook his head, his voice filled with regret. "I was scared, David. I thought I could handle it, that I could play both sides and protect my family. But it got out of hand."

David took a deep breath, trying to contain his anger. "You've put everything we've worked for at risk. The leaks, the setbacks – they've all been because of you. We trusted you, Carlos."

Carlos looked up, his eyes filled with tears. "I'm sorry, David. I never wanted to betray you. I was just trying to protect my family."

David felt a pang of sympathy but knew that he couldn't let emotions cloud his judgment. "We need to address this, Carlos. We can't let your actions jeopardize everything we've achieved. You'll need to step down, and we'll need to handle this internally before it becomes public."

Carlos nodded, his shoulders slumping in defeat. "I understand. I'll do whatever I can to make things right."

As Carlos left the office, David felt a mix of relief and sadness. The betrayal had been a harsh blow, but they had acted quickly and decisively. Now, they needed to focus on damage control and ensuring that their reforms continued to move forward.

The news of Carlos's resignation spread quickly, and speculation about the reasons behind it began to circulate. David and his team worked diligently to manage the narrative, emphasizing their commitment to transparency and integrity.

At a press conference, David addressed the situation head-on. "As many of you know, Carlos Mendoza has resigned from his position. We have reason to believe that he was coerced into cooperating with individuals who sought to undermine our efforts. While we are deeply saddened by this betrayal, we remain committed to our mission of creating a more just and equitable city. We will continue to fight for the people and ensure that those who abuse their power are held accountable."

The response from the public was mixed. Some were shocked and disheartened by the betrayal, while others admired David's transparency and determination to address the issue. The Power Brokers seized the opportunity to further attack David's administration, but the evidence against them continued to mount.

Despite the setback, David's administration pressed on with their reform agenda. They identified a capable replacement for Carlos and continued to engage with the community, building support for their initiatives. The investigation into the Power Brokers progressed, and more high-ranking officials were implicated in the scandal.

One evening, as David sat in his office reflecting on the events of the past few weeks, Rachel walked in with a thoughtful expression. "David, I've been thinking. This betrayal has been a major setback, but it's also an opportunity. We can use this to strengthen our commitment to transparency and accountability."

David nodded, appreciating Rachel's perspective. "You're right. We need to turn this into a positive. Let's double down on our efforts to engage with the community and build trust. We can't let this betrayal define us."

Rachel smiled, her eyes filled with determination. "We've faced bigger challenges before, and we've always come out stronger. We'll get through this too."

As the weeks passed, David's administration continued to make strides in advancing their reform agenda. The betrayal had been a harsh blow, but it had also reinforced their commitment to their mission. They worked tirelessly to build trust with the community, engaging with citizens through town hall meetings, public forums, and outreach initiatives.

One of the most significant victories came with the passage of new legislation to protect whistleblowers and ensure greater transparency in government. This reform was a direct response to the betrayal and aimed to prevent similar incidents in the future.

At the signing ceremony for the new legislation, David stood alongside Sarah Thompson, Rachel, Tom, and other key allies. The room was filled with community members, activists, and journalists who had fought tirelessly for this reform.

"Today marks a significant step forward in our fight for justice and integrity," David said, his voice filled with pride. "This legislation will protect those who come forward with information about corruption and ensure that our government remains transparent and accountable to the people it serves. It's a testament to what we can achieve when we come together to fight for what's right."

The applause was thunderous, and David felt a deep sense of fulfillment. The journey had been challenging, but moments like this reaffirmed his commitment to the cause.

Despite the ongoing attacks from the Power Brokers, David's administration continued to make strides in advancing their reform agenda. The betrayal had tested his resolve and his principles, but he remained resolute in his mission. He knew that the fight for a more just and equitable city was a long and arduous journey, but he was determined to see it through.

One evening, as David sat in his office reflecting on the journey so far, Rachel walked in with a smile on her face. "David, I have good news. The investigation into the Power Brokers is progressing, and several key members have been indicted. The tide is turning."

David felt a sense of relief and accomplishment. The battle was far from over, but they had made significant progress. "That's fantastic news, Rachel. We've come a long way, and we're making a real difference."

Rachel nodded, her eyes filled with determination. "We have, and we will continue to fight. This city deserves a government that truly serves its people. And we're going to make sure that happens."

David smiled, feeling a renewed sense of purpose. The journey had been challenging, and there were undoubtedly more obstacles ahead. But he knew that they were on the right path. The betrayal had been a turning point, and their commitment to transparency and accountability was stronger than ever.

As David looked out over the city once more, he felt a sense of hope. The skyline, once a symbol of ambition and burden, now represented the potential for genuine change. He had made a promise to the people, and he was determined to see it through.

The battle against the Power Brokers had tested his resolve and his principles, but David Collins was ready to face the challenges ahead. With the support of his allies and the community, he would continue to fight for a city that truly served its people. The path was clear, and the future looked brighter than ever before.

Chapter 8: The Scandal

David Collins walked into his office on a crisp autumn morning, the air filled with the promise of a new day. The skyline, bathed in the golden glow of the rising sun, looked almost serene—a stark contrast to the turbulence that lay ahead. Unbeknownst to David, the Power Brokers were about to launch their most audacious attack yet, aiming to bring him to his knees and reclaim their influence over the city.

Rachel and Tom were already in the conference room, poring over the latest reports and preparing for the day's meetings. As David entered, Rachel looked up, her face showing the strain of their relentless battle against corruption.

"Morning, David," she said, forcing a smile. "We've got a busy day ahead."

David nodded, sensing her unease. "What's going on, Rachel? You look worried."

Before Rachel could respond, Tom's phone buzzed with a notification. He glanced at the screen, and his face paled. "David, you need to see this," he said, handing over his phone.

David's eyes scanned the screen, taking in the headline that blared across the news site: "Mayor Collins Accused of Embezzlement: Shocking Revelations Uncovered."

David felt as if he'd been punched in the gut. "What the hell is this?" he muttered, scrolling through the article. It detailed allegations of financial misconduct, claiming that David had embezzled city funds for personal use. The article cited anonymous sources and presented what appeared to be damning evidence—bank statements, emails, and financial records.

"This is a smear campaign," David said, his voice trembling with anger. "The Power Brokers must be behind this. They forged these documents to discredit me."

Rachel nodded, her expression grim. "It looks that way, but we need to act fast. The media is going to run with this story, and we need to get ahead of it."

Tom was already on his phone, coordinating with their legal team. "We need to issue a statement and hold a press conference. We also need to gather evidence to refute these claims. If we can prove that the documents are forgeries, we can turn this around."

David took a deep breath, trying to steady his nerves. "Let's get to work. We need to clear my name and show the people that this is a baseless attack."

The next few hours were a whirlwind of activity. David's team worked tirelessly to gather evidence, contact allies, and prepare for the press conference. Emily Reyes, the investigative journalist who had been instrumental in their fight against the Power Brokers, arrived with her team, ready to assist.

"David, I've seen the article," Emily said, her voice filled with determination. "We're going to help you get to the bottom of this. I have sources who can help verify the authenticity of these documents."

David felt a surge of gratitude. "Thank you, Emily. We need all the help we can get. This is a coordinated attack, and we need to expose it for what it is."

As the day wore on, David's team uncovered several inconsistencies in the documents presented in the article. The bank statements contained errors that suggested they had been manipulated, and the emails were traced back to a server known for hosting fake accounts. It was clear that the Power Brokers had gone to great lengths to fabricate evidence and orchestrate the scandal.

By the time the press conference began, the room was packed with journalists, community leaders, and supporters. David stood at the podium, flanked by Rachel, Tom, and Emily. The atmosphere was tense, the air thick with anticipation.

"Good afternoon," David began, his voice steady but filled with emotion. "Today, I stand before you to address the allegations that have been made against me. These accusations are false, and they are part of a coordinated effort by the Power Brokers to undermine my credibility and control our city. I am here to present evidence that refutes these claims and to reaffirm my commitment to transparency and integrity."

He held up the forged documents, letting the cameras capture them. "Our team has uncovered several inconsistencies in these documents, which prove that they have been manipulated. The bank statements contain errors, and the emails were traced back to a server known for hosting fake accounts. This is a calculated attempt to discredit me and derail our efforts to bring about meaningful change."

Emily stepped forward, presenting her findings. "As an investigative journalist, I have verified the evidence presented here today. The documents used to accuse Mayor Collins are forgeries, created by those who seek to protect their own interests at the expense of the truth."

The room erupted into murmurs as the journalists processed the information. David continued, his voice filled with conviction. "I will not be intimidated by these tactics. We will continue to fight for justice and accountability, and we will not allow the Power Brokers to dictate the future of our city. I ask for your support as we work to uncover the truth and hold those responsible accountable."

The press conference had a profound impact, but the battle was far from over. The Power Brokers were relentless, using their influence to spread further misinformation and sow doubt about David's integrity. The media frenzy intensified, and the scandal dominated the headlines.

David and his team worked around the clock to manage the crisis. They engaged with the public through town hall meetings, social media, and community events, emphasizing their commitment to transparency and justice. They also continued to gather evidence, determined to expose the Power Brokers' involvement in orchestrating the scandal.

One evening, as David prepared for a live television interview, Rachel pulled him aside. "David, this interview is crucial. We need to counter the negative narrative and reinforce your message of integrity and reform. Be honest, be relatable, and don't let them rattle you."

David nodded, appreciating Rachel's unwavering support. "I know. We've come too far to let them derail us now."

The interview was conducted by a seasoned journalist known for her tough questions. David was prepared, but he knew that he needed to be on his toes.

"Mayor Collins, the allegations of embezzlement have shaken the public's confidence in your administration. How do you respond to claims that these accusations are part of a broader pattern of financial misconduct?" the journalist asked.

David took a deep breath, his expression resolute. "These allegations are baseless and part of a coordinated effort to discredit me and undermine our efforts to bring about meaningful change. We have presented evidence that proves the documents used to accuse me are forgeries. I am committed to transparency and accountability, and I will continue to fight for the truth and for the people of this city."

The journalist pressed on. "What about the impact on your administration's ability to govern? How do you plan to restore public trust and move forward?"

David shook his head. "The people elected me to serve them and to fight against corruption. We will continue to focus on our reform agenda and work to restore public trust through our actions. This administration remains committed to transparency, integrity, and justice. The challenges we face are significant, but I believe we are on the right path."

The interview continued, and David remained composed, addressing each question with clarity and conviction. By the end, he felt a sense of accomplishment, knowing that he had effectively communicated his message and countered the negative narrative.

Despite their efforts, the scandal took a toll on David and his team. The constant barrage of attacks and the need to constantly defend their integrity were exhausting. David often found himself questioning whether he could continue to fight this battle without compromising his values.

One evening, as David sat in his office feeling the weight of the ongoing struggle, Carlos Mendoza, the activist and community organizer who had been a steadfast ally, walked in.

"David, I know this has been tough," Carlos said, his voice filled with empathy. "But you need to remember why you started this journey. You're fighting for the people, for justice, and for a better future. Don't let the Power Brokers' tactics make you lose sight of that."

David nodded, grateful for Carlos's support. "I know, Carlos. It's just hard sometimes. The constant attacks, the ethical dilemmas... it's a lot to handle."

Carlos placed a hand on David's shoulder. "You're not alone in this fight. You have a team of dedicated people who believe in you and the work you're doing. And you have the support of the community. We'll get through this together."

David felt a renewed sense of determination. The scandal was a challenging and complex battleground, but he was not alone. With the support of his team, his allies, and the community, he would continue to fight for justice and integrity.

As the weeks passed, the investigation into the Power Brokers progressed, and more revelations about their corruption came to light. The authorities took swift action, and several high-ranking officials were indicted. The city's political landscape began to shift, and there was a renewed sense of hope and optimism among the citizens.

One of the most significant victories came with the passage of new legislation to increase transparency and accountability in government. These reforms were a direct response to the corruption exposed by the Power Brokers' activities, and they were a testament to David's commitment to creating a more just and equitable city.

At the signing ceremony for the new legislation, David stood alongside Sarah Thompson, Carlos Mendoza, and other key allies. The room was filled with community members, activists, and journalists who had fought tirelessly for this reform.

"Today marks a significant step forward in our fight for justice and integrity," David said, his voice filled with pride. "This legislation will ensure that our government remains transparent and accountable to the people it serves. It's a testament to what we can achieve when we come together to fight for what's right."

The applause was thunderous, and David felt a deep sense of fulfillment. The journey had been challenging, but moments like this reaffirmed his commitment to the cause.

Despite the ongoing attacks from the Power Brokers, David's administration continued to make strides in advancing their reform agenda. The scandal had tested his resolve and his principles, but he remained resolute in his mission. He knew that the fight for a more just and equitable city was a long and arduous journey, but he was determined to see it through.

One evening, as David sat in his office reflecting on the journey so far, Rachel walked in with a smile on her face. "David, I have good news. The investigation into the Power Brokers is progressing, and several key members have been indicted. The tide is turning."

David felt a sense of relief and accomplishment. The battle was far from over, but they had made significant progress. "That's fantastic news, Rachel. We've come a long way, and we're making a real difference."

Rachel nodded, her eyes filled with determination. "We have, and we will continue to fight. This city deserves a government that truly serves its people. And we're going to make sure that happens."

David smiled, feeling a renewed sense of purpose. The journey had been challenging, and there were undoubtedly more obstacles ahead. But he knew that they were on the right path. The scandal had been a turning point, and their commitment to transparency and accountability was stronger than ever.

As David looked out over the city once more, he felt a sense of hope. The skyline, once a symbol of ambition and burden, now represented the potential for genuine change. He had made a promise to the people, and he was determined to see it through.

The battle against the Power Brokers had tested his resolve and his principles, but David Collins was ready to face the challenges ahead. With the support of his allies and the community, he would continue to fight for a city that truly served its people. The path was clear, and the future looked brighter than ever before.

Chapter 9: The Grassroots Movement

David Collins leaned back in his chair, staring at the map of the city pinned to the wall of his office. Red pins marked areas of significant political and economic influence—strongholds of the Power Brokers. Blue pins indicated places where his administration had made progress in reform. Yet, there were many unmarked areas, neighborhoods and communities that had yet to feel the impact of his efforts.

The scandal orchestrated by the Power Brokers had been a brutal reminder of the entrenched power structures he was up against. Despite clearing his name, the constant battles were taking a toll, and David knew he needed a new approach. The traditional political avenues were not enough to dismantle the deep-rooted corruption. It was time for something different, something that bypassed the traditional power structures entirely.

The idea had been simmering in his mind for weeks: a grassroots movement, driven by the people, for the people. He envisioned a campaign that empowered citizens, fostered community leadership, and created a groundswell of support for genuine political reform. It was a bold and risky move, but it might be the only way to achieve lasting change.

David called an emergency meeting with his core team—Rachel, Tom, Sarah Thompson, and Carlos Mendoza. Emily Reyes, the investigative journalist, was also present. The atmosphere was charged with anticipation and curiosity.

"Thank you all for coming on such short notice," David began, his voice steady but filled with determination. "We've made significant progress in our fight against corruption, but it's clear that traditional political methods alone are not enough. The Power Brokers' influence is too entrenched. We need a new strategy, one that puts the power back in the hands of the people."

Rachel leaned forward, her eyes narrowing with interest. "What are you proposing, David?"

David took a deep breath. "A grassroots movement. We rally public support for genuine political reform, bypassing traditional power structures. We empower communities, foster local leadership, and create a groundswell of support that can't be ignored. This isn't just about politics—it's about changing the way our city operates from the ground up."

Tom raised an eyebrow. "It's a bold idea, David. But how do we start? And how do we sustain it?"

David nodded. "We start by engaging with the communities that have been most affected by corruption and neglect. We listen to their concerns, involve them in the decision-making process, and provide the resources they need to organize and lead. We use every tool at our disposal—social media, town hall meetings, community events—to build momentum. And we stay committed, no matter how tough it gets."

Sarah Thompson smiled, her eyes sparkling with excitement. "I love it, David. This is exactly what we need. I've seen how powerful grassroots movements can be. They can change the world."

Carlos Mendoza, who had been silent until now, nodded in agreement. "Count me in. I've been working with grassroots organizations for years. We can do this, David. We just need to be strategic and persistent."

Emily Reyes, always the skeptic, leaned back in her chair, her arms crossed. "It's ambitious, David. But it could work. If we can expose the Power Brokers and show the public what we're fighting for, we can build a movement that can't be stopped."

The decision was made. Over the next few days, David and his team worked tirelessly to develop a comprehensive plan for the grassroots movement. They reached out to community leaders, activists, and organizations, building a network of allies who shared their vision for reform.

The launch event was held in a large community center in one of the city's most underserved neighborhoods. The atmosphere was electric, with hundreds of people gathered to hear David speak. The room was filled with a diverse mix of citizens—young and old, activists and ordinary residents, all united by a desire for change.

David stepped up to the podium, feeling a surge of adrenaline. This was it—the beginning of a new chapter in their fight for justice and integrity.

"Good evening," David began, his voice resonating with passion. "Thank you all for being here tonight. Our city is at a crossroads. We have seen the impact of corruption and neglect, and we have fought hard to bring about change. But it's not enough. We need to do more. We need to take our fight to the next level. Tonight, we are launching a grassroots movement to reclaim our city from the forces that have held it back for too long. This movement is about empowering each and every one of you to become leaders and advocates for change. Together, we can create a city that truly serves its people."

The crowd erupted into applause, and David felt a swell of hope. He continued, outlining the goals and strategies of the movement. They would focus on key issues such as affordable housing, healthcare, education, and environmental justice. They would hold town hall meetings, organize community events, and use social media to spread their message and build support.

As the event concluded, David mingled with the attendees, shaking hands and listening to their stories. The energy in the room was palpable, and David knew they were on the right path.

Over the next few weeks, the grassroots movement gained momentum. David and his team held meetings in neighborhoods across the city, listening to residents' concerns and involving them in the decision-making process. They partnered with local organizations to provide resources and support, helping communities organize and advocate for their needs.

One of the movement's early successes came in the form of a campaign to address the issue of food deserts in the city's underserved areas. David's team worked with local farmers, businesses, and nonprofits to create community gardens and establish farmers' markets, providing fresh, affordable produce to residents who had previously lacked access to healthy food options.

At the grand opening of one such community garden, David stood alongside local leaders and residents, feeling a deep sense of accomplishment.

"This is what our movement is all about," David said, addressing the crowd. "It's about coming together to solve problems and create a better future for our communities. This garden is more than just a source of fresh food—it's a symbol of what we can achieve when we work together."

The grassroots movement continued to grow, and David's administration saw a surge in public support. However, the Power Brokers were not about to let their influence wane without a fight. They launched a series of counterattacks, using their media connections to spread misinformation and sow doubt about the movement's intentions.

One evening, as David prepared for a live television interview, Rachel pulled him aside. "David, the Power Brokers are ramping up their attacks. They're spreading rumors that our movement is a front for radical agendas. We need to address this head-on."

David nodded, appreciating Rachel's vigilance. "I know. We'll counter their lies with the truth. We've been transparent from the start, and we'll continue to be. The people know what we're fighting for."

The interview was conducted by a seasoned journalist known for her tough questions. David was prepared, but he knew that he needed to be on his toes.

"Mayor Collins, your grassroots movement has gained significant traction, but there are concerns about its true intentions. Some say it's a front for radical agendas. How do you respond to these accusations?" the journalist asked.

David took a deep breath, his expression resolute. "Our movement is about one thing: empowering the people of this city to create positive change. We are committed to transparency, integrity, and addressing the real issues that our communities face. The accusations being spread by our opponents are baseless and designed to distract from the real work we're doing. We will continue to focus on our goals and engage with the public to build a better future for our city."

The journalist pressed on. "What about the impact on your administration's ability to govern? How do you plan to maintain public trust and move forward?"

David shook his head. "The people elected me to serve them and to fight against corruption. We will continue to focus on our reform agenda and work to restore public trust through our actions. This administration remains committed to transparency, integrity, and justice. The challenges we face are significant, but I believe we are on the right path."

The interview continued, and David remained composed, addressing each question with clarity and conviction. By the end, he felt a sense of accomplishment, knowing that he had effectively communicated his message and countered the negative narrative.

Despite their efforts, the grassroots movement faced numerous challenges. The Power Brokers used their influence to undermine the movement at every turn, and the constant attacks took a toll on David and his team. But the support from the community was unwavering, and the movement continued to grow.

One of the movement's most significant achievements came in the form of a campaign to address the city's affordable housing crisis. David's team worked with local developers, nonprofits, and community leaders to create a comprehensive plan that included the construction of new affordable housing units, rental assistance programs, and measures to prevent displacement due to gentrification.

At a press conference announcing the plan, David stood alongside Sarah Thompson, Carlos Mendoza, and other key allies. The room was filled with community members, activists, and journalists who had fought tirelessly for this reform.

"Today marks a significant step forward in our fight for affordable housing," David said, his voice filled with pride. "This plan is the result of months of hard work and collaboration with our community. It will ensure that everyone in our city has a place to call home and that our neighborhoods remain vibrant and diverse. It's a testament to what we can achieve when we come together to fight for what's right."

The applause was thunderous, and David felt a deep sense of fulfillment. The journey had been challenging, but moments like this reaffirmed his commitment to the cause.

Despite the ongoing attacks from the Power Brokers, David's administration continued to make strides in advancing their reform agenda. The grassroots movement had breathed new life into their efforts, and the support from the community was stronger than ever.

One evening, as David sat in his office reflecting on the journey so far, Rachel walked in with a smile on her face. "David, I have good news. The investigation into the Power Brokers is progressing, and several key members have been indicted. The tide is turning."

David felt a sense of relief and accomplishment. The battle was far from over, but they had made significant progress. "That's fantastic news, Rachel. We've come a long way, and we're making a real difference."

Rachel nodded, her eyes filled with determination. "We have, and we will continue to fight. This city deserves a government that truly serves its people. And we're going to make sure that happens."

David smiled, feeling a renewed sense of purpose. The journey had been challenging, and there were undoubtedly more obstacles ahead. But he knew that they were on the right path. The grassroots movement had been a turning point, and their commitment to transparency and accountability was stronger than ever.

As David looked out over the city once more, he felt a sense of hope. The skyline, once a symbol of ambition and burden, now represented the potential for genuine change. He had made a promise to the people, and he was determined to see it through.

The battle against the Power Brokers had tested his resolve and his principles, but David Collins was ready to face the challenges ahead. With the support of his allies and the community, he would continue to fight for a city that truly served its people. The path was clear, and the future looked brighter than ever before.

The grassroots movement continued to gain momentum, with new initiatives and campaigns being launched regularly. David's administration focused on addressing key issues that had long been neglected, such as education reform, healthcare access, and environmental justice.

One of the movement's most impactful initiatives was a campaign to improve the quality of education in the city's public schools. David's team worked with teachers, parents, and community leaders to develop a comprehensive plan that included increased funding for schools, expanded access to early childhood education, and programs to support students' mental health and well-being.

At a town hall meeting to discuss the education reform plan, David stood before a packed auditorium, feeling the energy and excitement of the crowd.

"Thank you all for being here tonight," David began, his voice resonating with passion. "Education is the foundation of our future, and we must ensure that every child in our city has access to a high-quality education. Our plan is the result of extensive collaboration with educators, parents, and community leaders, and it represents a significant investment in our children's future."

The crowd erupted into applause, and David continued, outlining the key components of the plan and the steps they would take to implement it. He emphasized the importance of community involvement and encouraged residents to stay engaged and hold the administration accountable.

As the meeting concluded, David mingled with the attendees, shaking hands and listening to their stories. The enthusiasm and support from the community were palpable, and David knew they were on the right path.

The grassroots movement's efforts were not without challenges. The Power Brokers continued to launch attacks, using their influence to spread misinformation and undermine the movement's credibility. But David and his team remained resolute, countering the attacks with transparency and honesty.

One evening, as David prepared for another live television interview, Rachel pulled him aside. "David, the Power Brokers are stepping up their attacks. They're spreading rumors that our education reform plan is too costly and unrealistic. We need to address this head-on."

David nodded, appreciating Rachel's vigilance. "I know. We'll counter their lies with the truth. We've been transparent from the start, and we'll continue to be. The people know what we're fighting for."

The interview was conducted by a seasoned journalist known for her tough questions. David was prepared, but he knew that he needed to be on his toes.

"Mayor Collins, your grassroots movement has gained significant traction, but there are concerns about the feasibility of your education reform plan. Some say it's too costly and unrealistic. How do you respond to these accusations?" the journalist asked.

David took a deep breath, his expression resolute. "Our education reform plan is a necessary investment in our children's future. The accusations being spread by our opponents are baseless and designed to distract from the real work we're doing. We have outlined a clear and achievable plan, and we are committed to ensuring that every child in our city has access to a high-quality education. The challenges we face are significant, but I believe we are on the right path."

The journalist pressed on. "What about the impact on your administration's ability to govern? How do you plan to maintain public trust and move forward?"

David shook his head. "The people elected me to serve them and to fight against corruption. We will continue to focus on our reform agenda and work to restore public trust through our actions. This administration remains committed to transparency, integrity, and justice. The challenges we face are significant, but I believe we are on the right path."

The interview continued, and David remained composed, addressing each question with clarity and conviction. By the end, he felt a sense of accomplishment, knowing that he had effectively communicated his message and countered the negative narrative.

Despite their efforts, the grassroots movement faced numerous challenges. The Power Brokers used their influence to undermine the movement at every turn, and the constant attacks took a toll on David and his team. But the support from the community was unwavering, and the movement continued to grow.

One of the movement's most significant achievements came in the form of a campaign to address the city's environmental challenges. David's team worked with environmental organizations, community leaders, and local businesses to develop a comprehensive plan to reduce pollution, increase green spaces, and promote sustainable practices.

At a press conference announcing the environmental plan, David stood alongside Sarah Thompson, Carlos Mendoza, and other key allies. The room was filled with community members, activists, and journalists who had fought tirelessly for this reform.

"Today marks a significant step forward in our fight for environmental justice," David said, his voice filled with pride. "This plan is the result of months of hard work and collaboration with our community. It will ensure that our city remains a healthy and sustainable place for future generations. It's a testament to what we can achieve when we come together to fight for what's right."

The applause was thunderous, and David felt a deep sense of fulfillment. The journey had been challenging, but moments like this reaffirmed his commitment to the cause.

Despite the ongoing attacks from the Power Brokers, David's administration continued to make strides in advancing their reform agenda. The grassroots movement had breathed new life into their efforts, and the support from the community was stronger than ever.

One evening, as David sat in his office reflecting on the journey so far, Rachel walked in with a smile on her face. "David, I have good news. The investigation into the Power Brokers is progressing, and several key members have been indicted. The tide is turning."

David felt a sense of relief and accomplishment. The battle was far from over, but they had made significant progress. "That's fantastic news, Rachel. We've come a long way, and we're making a real difference."

Rachel nodded, her eyes filled with determination. "We have, and we will continue to fight. This city deserves a government that truly serves its people. And we're going to make sure that happens."

David smiled, feeling a renewed sense of purpose. The journey had been challenging, and there were undoubtedly more obstacles ahead. But he knew that they were on the right path. The grassroots movement had been a turning point, and their commitment to transparency and accountability was stronger than ever.

As David looked out over the city once more, he felt a sense of hope. The skyline, once a symbol of ambition and burden, now represented the potential for genuine change. He had made a promise to the people, and he was determined to see it through.

The battle against the Power Brokers had tested his resolve and his principles, but David Collins was ready to face the challenges ahead. With the support of his allies and the community, he would continue to fight for a city that truly served its people. The path was clear, and the future looked brighter than ever before.

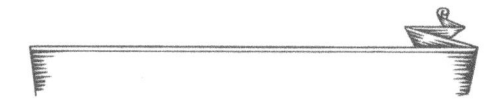

Chapter 10: The Threat

David Collins had always known that the fight for justice would be fraught with danger and opposition, but he hadn't anticipated just how personal and threatening it could become. The grassroots movement he had spearheaded was gaining momentum, and the public's support was unwavering. However, the Power Brokers, increasingly desperate to regain control, were about to take their campaign of intimidation and threats to a new, sinister level.

It began with small, unsettling incidents. One morning, as David and his wife, Julia, were leaving their home, they noticed that their car tires had been slashed. The act of vandalism was clearly a message, but David tried to downplay it to avoid worrying Julia and their two children, Emily and Jack. However, as the days passed, the threats escalated.

Late one evening, after a long day of meetings and community events, David received a chilling phone call. The voice on the other end was distorted, but the message was clear: "Back off, Collins, or you'll regret it."

David's heart raced, but he tried to remain calm. "Who is this? What do you want?"

The voice laughed coldly. "You're playing a dangerous game, Mayor. Think about your family. This is your only warning."

The line went dead, leaving David with a sense of dread. He immediately called Rachel and Tom, briefing them on the situation. They convened an emergency meeting with their security team to discuss the threats and take necessary precautions.

"David, this is serious," Rachel said, her face pale with concern. "We need to increase security for you and your family. We can't take any chances."

Tom nodded in agreement. "I've already contacted a private security firm. They'll have agents assigned to your home and family around the clock. We should also consider relocating you to a safer location temporarily."

David shook his head. "I won't be intimidated. We can't let them scare us into submission. We need to stay strong and continue our work."

Rachel placed a hand on his shoulder. "David, I understand your resolve, but we also need to be smart. Your safety and the safety of your family come first. We'll continue to fight, but we need to take these threats seriously."

David sighed, knowing she was right. "Okay. We'll take the necessary precautions. But we won't back down. We'll show them that we're not afraid."

As security measures were put in place, David struggled to balance his duties as mayor with the need to protect his family. The threats weighed heavily on his mind, but he remained focused on the grassroots movement and their goals. The public rallies, town hall meetings, and community events continued, each one reinforcing the support of the citizens and the momentum of the movement.

One evening, as David was preparing for a televised town hall meeting, he received a text message from an unknown number. It contained a photo of his children playing in their schoolyard, accompanied by the message: "They look so innocent. Be careful, David."

David's blood ran cold. He immediately called Julia, who reassured him that the children were safe and that the security team was with them. But the threat was clear—his enemies were willing to target his family to break his resolve.

At the town hall meeting, David addressed the crowd with his usual passion and determination, but inside, he was deeply troubled. After the event, as he was walking to his car, he was approached by a young woman with a look of desperation in her eyes.

"Mr. Mayor, I need to speak with you," she said urgently. "I have information about the Power Brokers. They're planning something big, and it's not just about you—it's about the entire city."

David gestured for his security detail to give them some space. "What do you know?"

The woman, who introduced herself as Lisa, explained that she had been working as an assistant to one of the key figures in the Power Brokers' network.

She had overheard conversations about plans to sabotage the city's infrastructure and create chaos to discredit David's administration.

"They're planning to attack the power grid and the water supply," Lisa said, her voice trembling. "They want to create a crisis that they can blame on you. If they succeed, it could endanger thousands of lives."

David listened intently, feeling a mix of anger and fear. "Thank you for coming forward, Lisa. Your information is invaluable. We'll take immediate action to prevent this."

As Lisa was escorted away by the security team, David called an emergency meeting with his top advisors and the heads of the city's critical infrastructure departments. They developed a plan to enhance security and monitor for any signs of sabotage.

The next few days were tense as they worked around the clock to safeguard the city's infrastructure. Meanwhile, David continued to receive threats, each one more menacing than the last. He knew that the Power Brokers were becoming increasingly desperate and dangerous.

One night, as David and Julia were having dinner with Emily and Jack, the security alarm at their home went off. The children looked frightened, and David quickly ushered them into a safe room while Julia called the security team. Moments later, the head of their security detail entered the house, his face serious.

"Mr. Collins, we've identified an intruder on the property. He's been apprehended, but we need to review the security footage to understand how he got past our defenses."

David's heart pounded as he followed the security chief to the monitoring room. The footage showed a masked figure cutting through the perimeter fence and making his way toward the house before being intercepted by the security team. It was a stark reminder of the lengths to which the Power Brokers were willing to go to intimidate him.

The next morning, David held a press conference to address the threats and the ongoing efforts to protect the city. He stood before the cameras, his expression resolute.

"Good morning," David began, his voice steady. "Over the past few weeks, my family and I have been subjected to threats and intimidation by those who seek to undermine our efforts to bring about positive change in our city. These threats are not just against me—they are against the very principles of justice and integrity that we stand for. We will not be intimidated. We will continue to fight for a better future for our city, and we will not allow fear to dictate our actions."

He paused, looking directly into the cameras. "To those who seek to harm us, know this: we are stronger than you think. We have the support of the people, and we will not back down. We will expose your corruption and bring you to justice."

The press conference was met with overwhelming support from the public. Messages of solidarity poured in, and David's resolve was further strengthened by the outpouring of encouragement. However, the Power Brokers' campaign of intimidation was far from over.

As David and his team continued to fortify the city's defenses, they also intensified their efforts to expose the Power Brokers' network. Emily Reyes, the investigative journalist, played a crucial role in uncovering new information and connecting the dots between various individuals and schemes.

One evening, as David was reviewing the latest findings with Emily, she shared a new lead that could potentially unravel the entire network. "David, we've identified a financial trail that links the Power Brokers to several offshore accounts. These accounts are used to launder money and fund their operations. If we can trace the transactions and expose the flow of funds, we can cripple their financial base."

David nodded, feeling a surge of hope. "This could be the breakthrough we need. Let's move quickly and gather all the evidence we can. We'll need to coordinate with federal authorities to take down these accounts and hold the perpetrators accountable."

The investigation into the financial trail required meticulous work and collaboration with international agencies. David and his team worked tirelessly, knowing that this could be their best chance to dismantle the Power Brokers' network once and for all.

As they closed in on the financial evidence, the threats against David and his family escalated. One night, as David was working late in his office, he received a text message from an unknown number. It contained a video of Julia and the children leaving their home, followed by a chilling message: "This is your final warning. Stop now, or you'll regret it."

David's hands shook with rage as he watched the video. He immediately called Julia, who assured him that they were safe and that the security team was with them. But the message was clear—the Power Brokers were willing to target his family to break his resolve.

David knew he couldn't back down. He called an emergency meeting with his core team and the heads of the security detail. "We need to increase security measures and ensure that my family is protected at all times," he said, his voice firm. "We also need to move quickly with our investigation. We can't let these threats stop us."

Rachel, ever the pragmatist, spoke up. "David, we need to be smart about this. The Power Brokers are getting desperate, and that makes them even more dangerous. We need to stay one step ahead and ensure that every move we make is calculated and precise."

Tom agreed. "We've come too far to let them win. We'll continue to gather evidence and coordinate with the authorities. But we also need to be prepared for any escalation in their tactics."

As the investigation progressed, David and his team uncovered more damning evidence linking the Power Brokers to various illegal activities. They worked closely with federal agencies to trace the financial transactions and build a comprehensive case against the network.

The breakthrough came when they identified a key figure within the Power Brokers' organization—a high-ranking official who had been orchestrating the financial schemes and coordinating the threats against David. With this information, they were able to secure warrants and initiate a series of raids on properties and accounts connected to the network.

The raids were a resounding success. Federal agents seized millions of dollars in assets, and several key members of the Power Brokers' network were arrested. The news sent shockwaves through the city, and the public's support for David's administration surged.

At a press conference to announce the arrests, David stood alongside federal officials, his expression resolute.

"Good evening," David began, his voice filled with determination. "Today, we have taken a significant step in our fight against corruption and intimidation. Thanks to the tireless efforts of our investigative team and the support of federal authorities, we have dismantled a major network of individuals who sought to undermine our city's integrity. This is a victory for justice, and it sends a clear message to those who seek to harm us: we will not be intimidated. We will continue to fight for a better future for our city, and we will not allow fear to dictate our actions."

The public response was overwhelmingly positive, with messages of support and gratitude pouring in from citizens across the city. David's resolve was further strengthened by the outpouring of encouragement, and he knew that their fight for justice was far from over.

Despite the success of the raids, the threats against David and his family continued. The Power Brokers, though weakened, were still a formidable force, and they were determined to retaliate. David and his team remained vigilant, knowing that the battle was not yet won.

One evening, as David was reviewing the latest security reports, he received a call from an unknown number. The voice on the other end was familiar—the same distorted voice that had threatened him before.

"You think you've won, Collins?" the voice sneered. "This is far from over. You may have taken down some of our people, but we'll be back. And next time, you won't see us coming."

David's grip tightened on the phone. "I'm not afraid of you. We will continue to fight, and we will bring you to justice."

The voice laughed coldly. "We'll see about that. Enjoy your victory while it lasts."

The line went dead, leaving David with a sense of unease. He knew that the Power Brokers were not bluffing, and that their fight was far from over. But he also knew that he couldn't let fear dictate his actions. He had come too far and sacrificed too much to back down now.

As the weeks passed, David and his team continued to fortify their efforts, both in terms of security and their ongoing investigations. They remained committed to their goals, knowing that the fight for justice was a long and arduous journey.

One evening, as David sat in his office reflecting on the journey so far, Rachel walked in with a smile on her face. "David, I have good news. The investigation into the Power Brokers is progressing, and several key members have been indicted. The tide is turning."

David felt a sense of relief and accomplishment. The battle was far from over, but they had made significant progress. "That's fantastic news, Rachel. We've come a long way, and we're making a real difference."

Rachel nodded, her eyes filled with determination. "We have, and we will continue to fight. This city deserves a government that truly serves its people. And we're going to make sure that happens."

David smiled, feeling a renewed sense of purpose. The journey had been challenging, and there were undoubtedly more obstacles ahead. But he knew that they were on the right path. The threats against him and his family had tested his resolve, but they had also strengthened his commitment to his mission.

As David looked out over the city once more, he felt a sense of hope. The skyline, once a symbol of ambition and burden, now represented the potential for genuine change. He had made a promise to the people, and he was determined to see it through.

The battle against the Power Brokers had tested his resolve and his principles, but David Collins was ready to face the challenges ahead. With the support of his allies and the community, he would continue to fight for a city that truly served its people. The path was clear, and the future looked brighter than ever before.

Chapter 11: The Conspiracy Unveiled

David Collins sat at his desk, staring at the piles of documents and digital files before him. The investigation into the Power Brokers had yielded a treasure trove of evidence, revealing a web of corruption and manipulation that extended far beyond what he had initially imagined. The scale of their influence was staggering, encompassing politicians, business leaders, law enforcement, and even elements within the media. Now, with the evidence in hand, David faced a monumental decision: how to unveil the conspiracy to the public without risking the safety of his team, his family, and the stability of the city.

The room was filled with the soft hum of computers and the quiet murmur of his most trusted advisors. Rachel, Tom, Sarah Thompson, Carlos Mendoza, and Emily Reyes had gathered for a critical meeting. The tension in the air was palpable, as they all knew the stakes were incredibly high.

"Thank you all for coming," David began, his voice steady but filled with urgency. "We have uncovered a vast conspiracy that has been controlling and corrupting our city for years. The evidence we have collected is damning, and we must decide how to present it to the public in a way that ensures maximum impact and minimal risk."

Rachel leaned forward, her brow furrowed with concern. "David, we need to be extremely careful. The Power Brokers are ruthless, and they will stop at nothing to protect themselves. We have to anticipate their moves and be ready for any counterattacks."

Tom nodded in agreement. "We need a multi-pronged approach. A public unveiling, backed by legal actions and media coverage. We have to hit them on all fronts simultaneously to prevent them from regrouping and launching a counteroffensive."

Sarah Thompson, the state senator and one of David's closest allies, spoke up. "I can help coordinate with our allies in the legislature and law enforcement. We need to ensure that the evidence is irrefutable and that the legal system is prepared to act swiftly."

Carlos Mendoza, the activist and community organizer, added, "We also need to rally public support. The people need to understand the gravity of the situation and why it's crucial to hold these individuals accountable. We can organize rallies and town hall meetings to keep the community informed and engaged."

Emily Reyes, the investigative journalist, had been instrumental in uncovering the conspiracy. She looked determined. "I'll work with my colleagues in the media to ensure comprehensive coverage. We need to control the narrative and prevent the Power Brokers from spreading misinformation."

David felt a surge of gratitude for his team's dedication and expertise. "Thank you, everyone. Let's divide the tasks and start executing the plan. Time is of the essence."

Over the next few days, the team worked tirelessly to compile and verify the evidence. They organized the documents, financial records, emails, and testimonies into a cohesive narrative that illustrated the full extent of the Power Brokers' corruption. Meanwhile, Sarah coordinated with lawmakers and law enforcement to prepare for the legal actions that would follow the public unveiling.

Carlos and his team mobilized community leaders and activists, organizing a series of rallies and town hall meetings to build public support. Emily worked with her colleagues to prepare a comprehensive media campaign that would ensure the story reached every corner of the city.

The day of the unveiling arrived, and the atmosphere was charged with anticipation. The event was held in a large auditorium, packed with journalists, community leaders, activists, and concerned citizens. The air was thick with tension, as everyone awaited the revelations that would soon be disclosed.

David stood at the podium, flanked by his team and key allies. The room fell silent as he began to speak.

"Good afternoon," David said, his voice steady but resonant with emotion. "Today, we stand at a critical juncture in our city's history. Over the past months, we have uncovered a vast conspiracy that has been manipulating and corrupting our political system, our economy, and our institutions. The individuals behind this conspiracy, known as the Power Brokers, have used their influence to enrich themselves at the expense of the people. Today, we are here to unveil the full extent of their corruption and to hold them accountable for their actions."

He paused, letting the weight of his words sink in. "The evidence we are about to present is irrefutable. It includes financial records, emails, testimonies, and other documents that clearly demonstrate the Power Brokers' illegal activities and manipulative tactics. We have coordinated with law enforcement and legal authorities to ensure that those responsible are brought to justice."

David then presented the evidence, piece by piece, detailing the Power Brokers' activities. He showed how they had manipulated elections, bribed officials, laundered money, and orchestrated smear campaigns against their opponents. He highlighted specific examples of their corruption, naming names and providing concrete proof of their wrongdoing.

As he spoke, the room erupted into murmurs of shock and outrage. The scale of the conspiracy was staggering, and the revelations were both compelling and damning. David continued, his voice growing stronger with each revelation.

"We will not allow these individuals to continue their reign of corruption. We will hold them accountable, and we will restore integrity to our city. This is not just a fight for justice—this is a fight for the soul of our community. We will not back down, and we will not be intimidated."

The applause was thunderous, and David felt a deep sense of fulfillment. The journey had been challenging, but moments like this reaffirmed his commitment to the cause.

The public unveiling was only the beginning. As the news spread, law enforcement agencies began to act on the evidence. Warrants were issued, arrests were made, and assets were seized. The Power Brokers' network began to unravel, and the city's political landscape started to shift.

Despite the success of the unveiling, David and his team remained vigilant. They knew that the Power Brokers would not go down without a fight. They anticipated counterattacks and worked tirelessly to stay one step ahead.

One evening, as David was reviewing the latest developments with Rachel and Tom, he received a call from Emily Reyes.

"David, we've received a tip that the Power Brokers are planning to retaliate. They may try to discredit us by planting false evidence or launching a smear campaign. We need to be prepared."

David nodded, his resolve unwavering. "We'll be ready, Emily. We've come too far to let them derail us now. We'll continue to fight, and we'll continue to expose the truth."

The following days were a whirlwind of activity as David and his team worked to fortify their efforts and counter any potential attacks. They remained focused on their goals, knowing that the fight for justice was a long and arduous journey.

One night, as David was working late in his office, he received an unexpected visit from Lisa, the former assistant who had provided crucial information about the Power Brokers' plans.

"David, I have more information," Lisa said, her voice urgent. "I've uncovered additional evidence that links the Power Brokers to several high-profile figures in the business and political world. This could be the final piece we need to bring them down."

David felt a surge of hope. "Thank you, Lisa. Your courage and determination have been invaluable. We'll use this information to strengthen our case and ensure that justice is served."

As the investigation continued, David and his team uncovered even more damning evidence. They worked closely with federal agencies to trace the financial transactions and build a comprehensive case against the Power Brokers' network.

The final breakthrough came when they identified a key figure within the organization—a high-ranking official who had been orchestrating the financial schemes and coordinating the threats against David. With this information, they were able to secure additional warrants and initiate a series of raids on properties and accounts connected to the network.

The raids were a resounding success. Federal agents seized millions of dollars in assets, and several key members of the Power Brokers' network were arrested. The news sent shockwaves through the city, and the public's support for David's administration surged.

At a press conference to announce the arrests, David stood alongside federal officials, his expression resolute.

"Good evening," David began, his voice filled with determination. "Today, we have taken a significant step in our fight against corruption and intimidation. Thanks to the tireless efforts of our investigative team and the support of federal authorities, we have dismantled a major network of individuals who sought to undermine our city's integrity. This is a victory for justice, and it sends a clear message to those who seek to harm us: we will not be intimidated. We will continue to fight for a better future for our city, and we will not allow fear to dictate our actions."

The public response was overwhelmingly positive, with messages of support and gratitude pouring in from citizens across the city. David's resolve was further strengthened by the outpouring of encouragement, and he knew that their fight for justice was far from over.

Despite the success of the raids, the threats against David and his family continued. The Power Brokers, though weakened, were still a formidable force, and they were determined to retaliate. David and his team remained vigilant, knowing that the battle was not yet won.

One evening, as David was reviewing the latest security reports, he received a call from an unknown number. The voice on the other end was familiar—the same distorted voice that had threatened him before.

"You think you've won, Collins?" the voice sneered. "This is far from over. You may have taken down some of our people, but we'll be back. And next time, you won't see us coming."

David's grip tightened on the phone. "I'm not afraid of you. We will continue to fight, and we will bring you to justice."

The voice laughed coldly. "We'll see about that. Enjoy your victory while it lasts."

The line went dead, leaving David with a sense of unease. He knew that the Power Brokers were not bluffing, and that their fight was far from over. But he also knew that he couldn't let fear dictate his actions. He had come too far and sacrificed too much to back down now.

As the weeks passed, David and his team continued to fortify their efforts, both in terms of security and their ongoing investigations. They remained committed to their goals, knowing that the fight for justice was a long and arduous journey.

One evening, as David sat in his office reflecting on the journey so far, Rachel walked in with a smile on her face. "David, I have good news. The investigation into the Power Brokers is progressing, and several key members have been indicted. The tide is turning."

David felt a sense of relief and accomplishment. The battle was far from over, but they had made significant progress. "That's fantastic news, Rachel. We've come a long way, and we're making a real difference."

Rachel nodded, her eyes filled with determination. "We have, and we will continue to fight. This city deserves a government that truly serves its people. And we're going to make sure that happens."

David smiled, feeling a renewed sense of purpose. The journey had been challenging, and there were undoubtedly more obstacles ahead. But he knew that they were on the right path. The unveiling of the conspiracy had been a turning point, and their commitment to transparency and accountability was stronger than ever.

As David looked out over the city once more, he felt a sense of hope. The skyline, once a symbol of ambition and burden, now represented the potential for genuine change. He had made a promise to the people, and he was determined to see it through.

The battle against the Power Brokers had tested his resolve and his principles, but David Collins was ready to face the challenges ahead. With the support of his allies and the community, he would continue to fight for a city that truly served its people. The path was clear, and the future looked brighter than ever before.

Chapter 12: The Assassination Attempt

David Collins awoke to the sound of his alarm, feeling a familiar mix of anticipation and determination. The day ahead was packed with meetings, public appearances, and strategic discussions aimed at further dismantling the Power Brokers' influence. The previous weeks had been a whirlwind of activity and progress, but David knew that the fight was far from over. He also knew that his enemies were becoming increasingly desperate and dangerous.

As he prepared for the day, Julia, his wife, entered the room with a worried expression. "David, are you sure you want to go through with today's events? The security team has been on high alert. They're concerned about potential threats."

David turned to her, placing a reassuring hand on her shoulder. "Julia, I can't let fear dictate my actions. We've come too far to back down now. The public needs to see that we're strong and committed to our cause."

Julia sighed, nodding reluctantly. "Just promise me you'll be careful."

"I promise," David said, kissing her forehead.

The day began with a series of meetings at City Hall, where David and his team discussed the next steps in their reform agenda. They were making significant progress, but the constant pressure and threats from the Power Brokers loomed large.

"David, we've received intelligence that there may be an increased risk of an attack today," Rachel said, her tone grave. "Our security detail is taking every precaution, but you need to stay vigilant."

David nodded, appreciating Rachel's concern. "I understand. We'll proceed with caution."

The morning meetings went smoothly, and by early afternoon, David was preparing for a major public appearance at a community center in one of the city's most underserved neighborhoods. The event was a crucial part of their grassroots movement, aimed at rallying public support and addressing key issues such as housing, education, and healthcare.

As David arrived at the community center, the atmosphere was electric. Hundreds of people had gathered to hear him speak, their faces filled with hope and anticipation. David felt a surge of pride and responsibility as he stepped onto the stage, flanked by his security detail and key allies.

"Good afternoon," David began, his voice carrying across the crowd. "Thank you all for being here today. Our city is at a crossroads, and we have a unique opportunity to create lasting change. Together, we can build a future that is just, equitable, and prosperous for everyone."

The crowd erupted into applause, and David continued, outlining the progress they had made and the challenges that lay ahead. He spoke passionately about the need for transparency, accountability, and community engagement, emphasizing the importance of working together to overcome obstacles.

As David spoke, he noticed a figure moving through the crowd, drawing closer to the stage. His instincts told him something was wrong, but he kept his focus on the speech, hoping that his security team was aware of the potential threat.

Just as David was wrapping up his speech, the figure suddenly pulled out a gun and aimed it at him. The crowd gasped in horror, and David's security detail sprang into action. Time seemed to slow down as the gunman fired, and David felt a sharp pain in his shoulder. He staggered, but his security team quickly surrounded him, shielding him from further harm.

"Get him to safety!" Rachel shouted, her voice filled with urgency.

David was rushed off the stage and into a waiting car, his shoulder throbbing with pain. He could hear the sounds of chaos and panic outside as the crowd reacted to the assassination attempt. The car sped away, sirens blaring, as David tried to process what had just happened.

"Are you okay?" Rachel asked, her face pale with worry.

David gritted his teeth, nodding. "I'll be fine. It's just a shoulder wound."

The car raced to the nearest hospital, where David was immediately taken to the emergency room. The medical team worked quickly to assess and treat his injuries, while his security detail and key advisors stood by, their faces etched with concern.

As David lay on the hospital bed, he felt a mix of anger, fear, and determination. The assassination attempt had been a stark reminder of the lengths to which the Power Brokers were willing to go to silence him. But he also knew that this attack would only strengthen his resolve and galvanize public support for their cause.

News of the assassination attempt spread rapidly, dominating headlines and social media. The public's reaction was immediate and intense, with messages of support and solidarity pouring in from across the city and beyond. The event had struck a chord with people, highlighting the high stakes of the fight for justice and integrity.

The hospital room was soon filled with visitors, including Julia and the children, who rushed to be by David's side. Julia's eyes were filled with tears as she embraced him, while Emily and Jack clung to his hands, their faces pale with worry.

"Daddy, are you going to be okay?" Emily asked, her voice trembling.

David smiled reassuringly. "I'm going to be fine, sweetheart. It's just a scratch."

Julia wiped away her tears, her voice filled with determination. "We're with you, David. No matter what happens, we'll stand by you."

David felt a surge of gratitude and love for his family. "Thank you. Your support means everything to me."

As the day progressed, David received visits from key allies, including Rachel, Tom, Sarah Thompson, Carlos Mendoza, and Emily Reyes. They discussed the implications of the assassination attempt and the steps they needed to take to ensure their safety while continuing their fight.

"We need to address the public as soon as possible," Rachel said, her tone firm. "They need to see that you're okay and that we're not backing down."

David nodded. "I agree. We'll hold a press conference here at the hospital. We need to show them that we're stronger than ever."

The press conference was organized swiftly, with journalists and camera crews gathering outside the hospital. David, with his shoulder bandaged and his face resolute, addressed the public from a wheelchair.

"Good evening," David began, his voice steady. "Earlier today, there was an attempt on my life. I want to assure you all that I am okay and that we will not be intimidated by this cowardly act. Our fight for justice and integrity will continue, and we will not let fear dictate our actions."

He paused, looking directly into the cameras. "To those who seek to silence us, know this: we are stronger than you think. We have the support of the people, and we will not back down. We will expose your corruption and bring you to justice. Our resolve is unshaken, and our commitment to creating a better future for our city is stronger than ever."

The press conference had a profound impact, galvanizing public opinion and increasing support for David's cause. The assassination attempt had highlighted the high stakes of their fight, and people rallied around David and his team, determined to see justice served.

In the days that followed, David's recovery was swift, thanks to the excellent medical care he received and the unwavering support of his family and friends. He remained in close contact with his team, coordinating their efforts and ensuring that their work continued unabated.

The investigation into the assassination attempt revealed that the gunman had ties to the Power Brokers' network. This connection provided further evidence of the lengths to which the organization was willing to go to protect their interests and silence their opponents.

As David's team worked closely with law enforcement to dismantle the Power Brokers' network, they also focused on strengthening their security measures and ensuring the safety of everyone involved. The public's support remained steadfast, and the grassroots movement continued to gain momentum.

One evening, as David was resting at home with Julia and the children, Rachel and Tom arrived with important updates.

"David, we've made significant progress in the investigation," Rachel said, her expression determined. "Several key members of the Power Brokers' network have been arrested, and we've uncovered more evidence of their illegal activities."

Tom nodded in agreement. "We're also seeing a surge in public support. The assassination attempt has galvanized people and increased their resolve to fight against corruption. We need to capitalize on this momentum and continue pushing forward."

David felt a sense of renewed purpose. "Thank you, both. We're making a real difference, and we can't let up now. Let's continue to expose the truth and hold those responsible accountable."

The following weeks were a whirlwind of activity as David and his team intensified their efforts. They worked closely with federal agencies to trace financial transactions, gather testimonies, and build a comprehensive case against the Power Brokers' network. Public rallies, town hall meetings, and community events were held regularly, keeping the citizens informed and engaged.

One of the movement's most significant achievements came in the form of a campaign to address the city's affordable housing crisis. David's team worked with local developers, nonprofits, and community leaders to create a comprehensive plan that included the construction of new affordable housing units, rental assistance programs, and measures to prevent displacement due to gentrification.

At a press conference announcing the plan, David stood alongside Sarah Thompson, Carlos Mendoza, and other key allies. The room was filled with community members, activists, and journalists who had fought tirelessly for this reform.

"Today marks a significant step forward in our fight for affordable housing," David said, his voice filled with pride. "This plan is the result of months of hard work and collaboration with our community. It will ensure that everyone in our city has a place to call home and that our neighborhoods remain vibrant and diverse. It's a testament to what we can achieve when we come together to fight for what's right."

The applause was thunderous, and David felt a deep sense of fulfillment. The journey had been challenging, but moments like this reaffirmed his commitment to the cause.

Despite the ongoing attacks from the Power Brokers, David's administration continued to make strides in advancing their reform agenda.

The assassination attempt had tested his resolve and his principles, but he remained resolute in his mission. He

knew that the fight for a more just and equitable city was a long and arduous journey, but he was determined to see it through.

One evening, as David sat in his office reflecting on the journey so far, Rachel walked in with a smile on her face. "David, I have good news. The investigation into the Power Brokers is progressing, and several key members have been indicted. The tide is turning."

David felt a sense of relief and accomplishment. The battle was far from over, but they had made significant progress. "That's fantastic news, Rachel. We've come a long way, and we're making a real difference."

Rachel nodded, her eyes filled with determination. "We have, and we will continue to fight. This city deserves a government that truly serves its people. And we're going to make sure that happens."

David smiled, feeling a renewed sense of purpose. The journey had been challenging, and there were undoubtedly more obstacles ahead. But he knew that they were on the right path. The assassination attempt had been a turning point, and their commitment to transparency and accountability was stronger than ever.

As David looked out over the city once more, he felt a sense of hope. The skyline, once a symbol of ambition and burden, now represented the potential for genuine change. He had made a promise to the people, and he was determined to see it through.

The battle against the Power Brokers had tested his resolve and his principles, but David Collins was ready to face the challenges ahead. With the support of his allies and the community, he would continue to fight for a city that truly served its people. The path was clear, and the future looked brighter than ever before.

The attempt on his life had not only failed to silence him but had also galvanized a movement that was now unstoppable. The people were more united than ever, and the push for reform had taken on a new urgency. David and his team knew that the coming months would be critical, but they were ready to face whatever challenges lay ahead.

The assassination attempt had been a stark reminder of the dangers they faced, but it had also strengthened their resolve. David knew that they were on the right side of history, and with the unwavering support of the community, they would continue their fight for justice and integrity.

The journey ahead was uncertain, but David Collins was determined to see it through. The people had placed their trust in him, and he would not let them down. The future of the city depended on their success, and David was committed to ensuring that the promise of a better tomorrow became a reality.

Chapter 13: The Showdown

The days following the assassination attempt were a blur of activity and heightened security. David Collins had emerged stronger and more determined than ever, with the public solidly behind him. The Power Brokers were now on the defensive, but they remained a formidable opponent. The final battle was approaching, and it would take place on a national stage.

David knew that the time had come to confront the Power Brokers directly, not just in the courts or through investigative journalism, but in the arena of public opinion. A televised debate had been arranged, where David would face off against a key representative of the Power Brokers. The stakes were incredibly high, and the outcome would shape the future of the city—and possibly the nation.

The preparations for the debate were intense. David and his team spent countless hours reviewing evidence, practicing arguments, and strategizing. They knew that this was their chance to expose the full extent of the Power Brokers' corruption and manipulative tactics to a national audience.

As the day of the debate approached, the tension in the air was palpable. The city was buzzing with anticipation, and the media was abuzz with speculation. The debate would be broadcast live across the country, and millions of people would be watching.

On the morning of the debate, David met with his core team—Rachel, Tom, Sarah Thompson, Carlos Mendoza, and Emily Reyes. They gathered in a conference room, reviewing their final preparations.

"David, this is it," Rachel said, her voice steady but filled with intensity. "Everything we've worked for has led to this moment. We need to make sure that we present our case clearly and convincingly. The Power Brokers will be prepared, and they'll use every trick in the book to try to undermine you."

Tom nodded. "We've identified their key points of attack. They'll likely try to discredit you personally, downplay the evidence, and shift the blame. We need to stay focused and keep the conversation centered on the facts."

Sarah Thompson, the state senator who had been a steadfast ally, spoke up. "I'll be in the audience, along with other supporters. We'll be ready to provide backup and respond to any attempts to disrupt the debate."

Carlos Mendoza added, "We've mobilized community leaders and activists to rally support. The public is with us, David. We just need to give them the truth."

Emily Reyes, the investigative journalist who had played a crucial role in uncovering the Power Brokers' activities, leaned forward. "I've provided you with the most damning evidence we have. Use it wisely. This is our chance to expose them once and for all."

David felt a surge of gratitude for his team's dedication and expertise. "Thank you, everyone. We're in this together. Let's make sure we leave no doubt about who the real villains are."

As the team dispersed to make final preparations, David took a moment to center himself. He knew that the debate would be a test of his resolve, his knowledge, and his ability to communicate the truth. But he also knew that he had the support of the people, and that gave him strength.

The debate was held in a large auditorium, packed with journalists, community leaders, activists, and concerned citizens. The atmosphere was charged with anticipation as David took the stage, facing off against Robert Hawthorne, a prominent business mogul and one of the key figures in the Power Brokers' network.

The moderator, a well-respected journalist, introduced the debate. "Good evening, ladies and gentlemen. Tonight, we have a critical debate between Mayor David Collins and Mr. Robert Hawthorne. The topic of discussion is the ongoing investigation into corruption and manipulation within our city's political and economic systems. Each participant will have the opportunity to present their case and respond to questions. Let's begin."

David and Hawthorne shook hands, the tension between them palpable. David could see the cold determination in Hawthorne's eyes, but he remained calm and focused.

The moderator turned to David. "Mayor Collins, you have the floor. Please begin with your opening statement."

David took a deep breath and began. "Thank you. Over the past months, my administration and our investigative team have uncovered extensive evidence of corruption and manipulation orchestrated by a group known as the Power Brokers. This group has used its influence to enrich itself at the expense of the people, undermining our political system and eroding public trust. Tonight, I will present this evidence and demonstrate the need for comprehensive reform to restore integrity and accountability to our city."

He paused, letting his words sink in. "Our fight is not just about politics—it's about justice and the future of our community. We cannot allow a small group of powerful individuals to dictate our destiny. We must stand together and demand change."

The moderator nodded and turned to Hawthorne. "Mr. Hawthorne, your opening statement."

Hawthorne smiled, his demeanor polished and confident. "Thank you. Mayor Collins has made serious accusations, but I believe they are based on misinformation and political grandstanding. The so-called evidence he presents is circumstantial at best, and his attempts to vilify successful business leaders like myself are nothing more than a distraction from his own administration's failures. Tonight, I will show that these allegations are unfounded and that Mayor Collins's actions are driven by a personal vendetta rather than the best interests of our city."

The audience was silent, the tension thick in the air. The debate had begun, and both sides were ready to fight for their narrative.

The moderator opened the floor for questions, starting with David. "Mayor Collins, can you provide specific examples of the corruption you allege and the evidence supporting these claims?"

David nodded, prepared for this moment. "Absolutely. Our investigation has uncovered multiple instances of bribery, money laundering, and manipulation of public contracts. For example, we have documented evidence of financial transactions between Mr. Hawthorne's companies and offshore accounts used to launder money. We have emails and recorded conversations showing direct involvement in bribing public officials to secure favorable contracts."

He held up a stack of documents, which were displayed on large screens for the audience to see. "These documents include financial records, emails, and testimonies from whistleblowers. They clearly demonstrate a pattern of illegal activities designed to enrich the Power Brokers at the expense of the public."

The moderator turned to Hawthorne. "Mr. Hawthorne, your response?"

Hawthorne's smile remained, but there was a hint of tension in his eyes. "These documents are taken out of context and do not prove any wrongdoing. Mayor Collins is using them to distract from his own administration's failures and to attack successful business leaders. The financial transactions he mentions are standard business practices, and the emails are selectively edited to fit his narrative."

David interjected. "Standard business practices do not include bribery and money laundering, Mr. Hawthorne. The evidence speaks for itself."

Hawthorne's composure wavered slightly. "These allegations are politically motivated and designed to undermine confidence in the business community. Mayor Collins is using his position to launch a personal attack on me and others who have contributed to the city's economic growth."

The moderator intervened. "Let's move to the next question. Mayor Collins, what steps do you propose to address the corruption you have identified?"

David took a deep breath. "We need comprehensive reforms to ensure transparency, accountability, and integrity in our political and economic systems. This includes stricter regulations on campaign financing, independent oversight of public contracts, and protections for whistleblowers. We must also strengthen our legal framework to ensure that those who engage in corrupt activities are held accountable. These reforms are essential to restoring public trust and creating a fair and just society."

The moderator turned to Hawthorne. "Mr. Hawthorne, your response?"

Hawthorne shook his head. "Mayor Collins's proposals are unrealistic and will stifle economic growth. His focus on punishment and regulation will create a hostile environment for businesses and drive away investment. What we need are policies that encourage innovation and growth, not a witch hunt against successful individuals."

David responded firmly. "Accountability and transparency are not antithetical to economic growth. In fact, they are essential for sustainable development. When businesses operate ethically and government functions transparently, everyone benefits. The current system, corrupted by the Power Brokers, only serves a privileged few at the expense of the many."

The debate continued, with David presenting detailed evidence and countering Hawthorne's arguments with calm determination. The tension in the room was palpable, but David remained focused, knowing that this was his chance to expose the truth to a national audience.

As the debate neared its conclusion, the moderator asked each participant to make a closing statement. David went first.

"Tonight, we have laid bare the corruption that has plagued our city for too long," he began, his voice resonant with conviction. "The evidence is clear, and the need for change is undeniable. This is not about politics—it's about justice and the future of our community. We must stand together and demand accountability from those who have abused their power. Together, we can build a city that is fair, just, and prosperous for everyone. I urge you all to join us in this fight for a better future."

The audience erupted into applause, their support and enthusiasm palpable. David felt a surge of hope and determination, knowing that they were on the right path.

Hawthorne's closing statement was filled with defiance. "Mayor Collins's accusations are baseless, and his proposals are misguided. We must focus on policies that encourage economic growth and innovation, not a witch hunt against successful individuals. I urge you to see through his political grandstanding and to support leaders who are committed to building a strong and prosperous city."

The debate concluded, and the audience filed out of the auditorium, buzzing with discussion and analysis. The media coverage was extensive, with pundits and commentators dissecting every moment of the showdown.

David and his team gathered in a private room, exhausted but exhilarated. They knew that the debate had been a pivotal moment, and the public's response was overwhelmingly positive.

"David, you did it," Rachel said, her voice filled with pride. "You exposed the truth and stood your ground. The public is with us."

Tom nodded. "The evidence you presented was compelling, and you countered Hawthorne's arguments effectively. We've turned the tide."

Sarah Thompson added, "We need to capitalize on this momentum. The public is engaged, and we have a unique opportunity to push for the reforms we need."

Carlos Mendoza spoke up. "We've mobilized community leaders and activists. The grassroots movement is stronger than ever, and people are ready to take action."

Emily Reyes, ever the pragmatist, added, "We need to continue our investigation and gather even more evidence. The Power Brokers won't give up easily, and we need to stay one step ahead."

David felt a surge of gratitude for his team's dedication and expertise. "Thank you, everyone. We've made significant progress, but our work is far from over. Let's continue to fight for justice and ensure that the truth prevails."

Over the next few weeks, David and his team intensified their efforts. They worked closely with law enforcement to follow up on the evidence presented during the debate, leading to several high-profile arrests and indictments. The public rallies, town hall meetings, and community events continued, with people from all walks of life joining the movement for reform.

One of the movement's most significant achievements came in the form of a campaign to address the city's environmental challenges. David's team worked with environmental organizations, community leaders, and local businesses to develop a comprehensive plan to reduce pollution, increase green spaces, and promote sustainable practices.

At a press conference announcing the environmental plan, David stood alongside Sarah Thompson, Carlos Mendoza, and other key allies. The room was filled with community members, activists, and journalists who had fought tirelessly for this reform.

"Today marks a significant step forward in our fight for environmental justice," David said, his voice filled with pride. "This plan is the result of months of hard work and collaboration with our community. It will ensure that our city remains a healthy and sustainable place for future generations. It's a testament to what we can achieve when we come together to fight for what's right."

The applause was thunderous, and David felt a deep sense of fulfillment. The journey had been challenging, but moments like this reaffirmed his commitment to the cause.

Despite the ongoing attacks from the Power Brokers, David's administration continued to make strides in advancing their reform agenda. The public debate had been a turning point, galvanizing support and increasing awareness of the need for change.

One evening, as David sat in his office reflecting on the journey so far, Rachel walked in with a smile on her face. "David, I have good news. The investigation into the Power Brokers is progressing, and several key members have been indicted. The tide is turning."

David felt a sense of relief and accomplishment. The battle was far from over, but they had made significant progress. "That's fantastic news, Rachel. We've come a long way, and we're making a real difference."

Rachel nodded, her eyes filled with determination. "We have, and we will continue to fight. This city deserves a government that truly serves its people. And we're going to make sure that happens."

David smiled, feeling a renewed sense of purpose. The journey had been challenging, and there were undoubtedly more obstacles ahead. But he knew that they were on the right path. The public debate had been a turning point, and their commitment to transparency and accountability was stronger than ever.

As David looked out over the city once more, he felt a sense of hope. The skyline, once a symbol of ambition and burden, now represented the potential for genuine change. He had made a promise to the people, and he was determined to see it through.

The battle against the Power Brokers had tested his resolve and his principles, but David Collins was ready to face the challenges ahead. With the support of his allies and the community, he would continue to fight for a city that truly served its people. The path was clear, and the future looked brighter than ever before.

Chapter 14: The Collapse

David Collins stood on the balcony of his office, gazing out over the city that had been both his battleground and his beacon of hope. The fight against the Power Brokers had been long and arduous, but the tide was finally turning. The recent televised debate had galvanized public opinion, and the momentum was now firmly on David's side. The once untouchable empire of the Power Brokers was beginning to crumble, and the people were demanding accountability and transparency like never before.

The morning sunlight cast a warm glow across the skyline, and David felt a renewed sense of purpose. He knew that the days ahead would be critical, but he also knew that they were on the right path. The collapse of the Power Brokers' network was not just a possibility—it was becoming a reality.

David's thoughts were interrupted by a knock on the door. Rachel entered, her face lit with a mixture of excitement and determination.

"David, we've received reports that several high-profile politicians and officials are defecting to our side," she said, handing him a stack of documents. "They're disillusioned with the Power Brokers and are ready to support our reform agenda."

David scanned the documents, his heart racing with anticipation. "This is incredible news, Rachel. It seems like the debate has had a profound impact. People are finally seeing the truth."

Rachel nodded. "Yes, and the public's demand for accountability is growing louder. We've been receiving countless messages of support and calls for action. The time is ripe for real change."

David felt a surge of hope. "Let's make sure we capitalize on this momentum. We need to continue to expose the corruption and push for the reforms we've been advocating for."

The day began with a series of meetings at City Hall, where David and his team strategized their next moves. The recent defections had created an opportunity to introduce and pass new legislation aimed at increasing transparency and accountability in government.

Tom, David's communications director, entered the room with a determined look on his face. "David, we need to hold a press conference to announce the defections and outline our next steps. The public needs to know that their demands are being heard and that we're taking action."

David agreed. "Absolutely. Let's organize the press conference for this afternoon. We'll present the new evidence we've gathered and highlight the support we're receiving from these defectors."

The press conference was held in a large auditorium, packed with journalists, community leaders, activists, and concerned citizens. The atmosphere was charged with anticipation as David took the stage, flanked by his team and several high-profile defectors.

"Good afternoon," David began, his voice resonating with conviction. "Today, we stand at a pivotal moment in our city's history. Over the past months, we have uncovered extensive evidence of corruption and manipulation orchestrated by the Power Brokers. This group has used its influence to enrich itself at the expense of the people, undermining our political system and eroding public trust. The recent defections of several high-profile politicians and officials to our side are a testament to the growing disillusionment with this corrupt network."

He paused, letting his words sink in. "We are here to announce a series of new reforms aimed at increasing transparency and accountability in government. These reforms include stricter regulations on campaign financing, independent oversight of public contracts, and protections for whistleblowers. We will ensure that those who engage in corrupt activities are held accountable."

The crowd erupted into applause, their support and enthusiasm palpable. David continued, outlining the specific measures they would take and emphasizing the importance of community involvement in the process.

"Together, we can build a city that is fair, just, and prosperous for everyone," David said. "We cannot allow a small group of powerful individuals to dictate our destiny. We must stand together and demand change."

As the press conference concluded, David mingled with the attendees, shaking hands and listening to their stories. The energy in the room was electric, and David knew that they were on the right path.

Over the next few weeks, the momentum continued to build. The defections had a ripple effect, with more politicians and officials coming forward to support David's reform agenda. The public's demand for accountability grew louder, and the pressure on the Power Brokers intensified.

One evening, as David was reviewing the latest developments with Rachel and Tom, he received a call from Emily Reyes, the investigative journalist who had been instrumental in uncovering the Power Brokers' activities.

"David, I've got more information," Emily said, her voice urgent. "We've uncovered additional evidence that links several key figures in the Power Brokers' network to illegal activities, including money laundering and bribery. This could be the final piece we need to bring them down."

David felt a surge of hope. "Thank you, Emily. Your work has been invaluable. We'll use this information to strengthen our case and ensure that justice is served."

As the investigation continued, David and his team worked closely with law enforcement to trace financial transactions, gather testimonies, and build a comprehensive case against the Power Brokers' network. The evidence they uncovered was damning, and the public's demand for action grew louder.

The collapse of the Power Brokers' empire was becoming increasingly apparent. High-profile arrests and indictments made headlines, and the once-powerful network began to unravel. The public rallies, town hall meetings, and community events continued, with people from all walks of life joining the movement for reform.

One of the movement's most significant achievements came in the form of a campaign to address the city's affordable housing crisis. David's team worked with local developers, nonprofits, and community leaders to create a comprehensive plan that included the construction of new affordable housing units, rental assistance programs, and measures to prevent displacement due to gentrification.

At a press conference announcing the plan, David stood alongside Sarah Thompson, Carlos Mendoza, and other key allies. The room was filled with community members, activists, and journalists who had fought tirelessly for this reform.

"Today marks a significant step forward in our fight for affordable housing," David said, his voice filled with pride. "This plan is the result of months of hard work and collaboration with our community. It will ensure that everyone in our city has a place to call home and that our neighborhoods remain vibrant and diverse. It's a testament to what we can achieve when we come together to fight for what's right."

The applause was thunderous, and David felt a deep sense of fulfillment. The journey had been challenging, but moments like this reaffirmed his commitment to the cause.

Despite the ongoing attacks from the Power Brokers, David's administration continued to make strides in advancing their reform agenda. The public's demand for accountability and transparency was stronger than ever, and the collapse of the Power Brokers' network was accelerating.

One evening, as David sat in his office reflecting on the journey so far, Rachel walked in with a smile on her face. "David, I have good news. The investigation into the Power Brokers is progressing, and several key members have been indicted. The tide is turning."

David felt a sense of relief and accomplishment. The battle was far from over, but they had made significant progress. "That's fantastic news, Rachel. We've come a long way, and we're making a real difference."

Rachel nodded, her eyes filled with determination. "We have, and we will continue to fight. This city deserves a government that truly serves its people. And we're going to make sure that happens."

David smiled, feeling a renewed sense of purpose. The journey had been challenging, and there were undoubtedly more obstacles ahead. But he knew that they were on the right path. The collapse of the Power Brokers' empire was a testament to the power of truth and the resilience of the human spirit.

As David looked out over the city once more, he felt a sense of hope. The skyline, once a symbol of ambition and burden, now represented the potential for genuine change. He had made a promise to the people, and he was determined to see it through.

The battle against the Power Brokers had tested his resolve and his principles, but David Collins was ready to face the challenges ahead. With the support of his allies and the community, he would continue to fight for a city that truly served its people. The path was clear, and the future looked brighter than ever before.

The following weeks were marked by a series of significant events that further accelerated the collapse of the Power Brokers' empire. David's administration introduced a series of legislative measures aimed at increasing transparency and accountability in government. These measures included stricter regulations on campaign financing, independent oversight of public contracts, and enhanced protections for whistleblowers.

The public's response was overwhelmingly positive. Citizens rallied around David's efforts, attending public meetings, signing petitions, and participating in grassroots campaigns to support the proposed reforms. The media coverage was extensive, with journalists highlighting the significance of the changes and the impact they would have on the city's governance.

One of the most impactful reforms was the establishment of an independent anti-corruption commission. This commission, composed of respected legal experts, community leaders, and former law enforcement officials, was tasked with investigating and prosecuting cases of corruption within the government and the private sector.

At the inauguration ceremony for the commission, David stood alongside key allies, addressing a crowd of supporters and media representatives.

"Today marks a historic moment in our fight for justice and integrity," David said, his voice filled with conviction. "The establishment of this independent anti-corruption commission is a critical step toward ensuring that our government remains transparent and accountable to the people it serves. This commission will have the authority to investigate and prosecute cases of corruption, holding those who abuse their power accountable. Together, we can build a city that is fair, just, and prosperous for everyone."

The applause was deafening, and David felt a deep sense of fulfillment. The journey had been challenging, but moments like this reaffirmed his commitment to the cause.

Despite the ongoing attacks from the Power Brokers, David's administration continued to make strides in advancing their reform agenda. The collapse of the Power Brokers' network was accelerating, with more high-profile arrests and indictments making headlines.

One evening, as David was reviewing the latest developments with Rachel and Tom, he received a call from Emily Reyes.

"David, I've got more information," Emily said, her voice urgent. "We've uncovered additional evidence that links several key figures in the Power Brokers' network to illegal activities, including money laundering and bribery. This could be the final piece we need to bring them down."

David felt a surge of hope. "Thank you, Emily. Your work has been invaluable. We'll use this information to strengthen our case and ensure that justice is served."

As the investigation continued, David and his team worked closely with law enforcement to trace financial transactions, gather testimonies, and build a comprehensive case against the Power Brokers' network. The evidence they uncovered was damning, and the public's demand for action grew louder.

The collapse of the Power Brokers' empire was becoming increasingly apparent. High-profile arrests and indictments made headlines, and the once-powerful network began to unravel. The public rallies, town hall meetings, and community events continued, with people from all walks of life joining the movement for reform.

One of the movement's most significant achievements came in the form of a campaign to address the city's environmental challenges. David's team worked with environmental organizations, community leaders, and local businesses to develop a comprehensive plan to reduce pollution, increase green spaces, and promote sustainable practices.

At a press conference announcing the environmental plan, David stood alongside Sarah Thompson, Carlos Mendoza, and other key allies. The room was filled with community members, activists, and journalists who had fought tirelessly for this reform.

"Today marks a significant step forward in our fight for environmental justice," David said, his voice filled with pride. "This plan is the result of months of hard work and collaboration with our community. It will ensure that our city remains a healthy and sustainable place for future generations. It's a testament to what we can achieve when we come together to fight for what's right."

The applause was thunderous, and David felt a deep sense of fulfillment. The journey had been challenging, but moments like this reaffirmed his commitment to the cause.

Despite the ongoing attacks from the Power Brokers, David's administration continued to make strides in advancing their reform agenda. The public's demand for accountability and transparency was stronger than ever, and the collapse of the Power Brokers' network was accelerating.

One evening, as David sat in his office reflecting on the journey so far, Rachel walked in with a smile on her face. "David, I have good news. The investigation into the Power Brokers is progressing, and several key members have been indicted. The tide is turning."

David felt a sense of relief and accomplishment. The battle was far from over, but they had made significant progress. "That's fantastic news, Rachel. We've come a long way, and we're making a real difference."

Rachel nodded, her eyes filled with determination. "We have, and we will continue to fight. This city deserves a government that truly serves its people. And we're going to make sure that happens."

David smiled, feeling a renewed sense of purpose. The journey had been challenging, and there were undoubtedly more obstacles ahead. But he knew that they were on the right path. The collapse of the Power Brokers' empire was a testament to the power of truth and the resilience of the human spirit.

As David looked out over the city once more, he felt a sense of hope. The skyline, once a symbol of ambition and burden, now represented the potential for genuine change. He had made a promise to the people, and he was determined to see it through.

The battle against the Power Brokers had tested his resolve and his principles, but David Collins was ready to face the challenges ahead. With the support of his allies and the community, he would continue to fight for a city that truly served its people. The path was clear, and the future looked brighter than ever before.

The following weeks were marked by a series of significant events that further accelerated the collapse of the Power Brokers' empire. David's administration introduced a series of legislative measures aimed at increasing transparency and accountability in government. These measures included stricter regulations on campaign financing, independent oversight of public contracts, and enhanced protections for whistleblowers.

The public's response was overwhelmingly positive. Citizens rallied around David's efforts, attending public meetings, signing petitions, and participating in grassroots campaigns to support the proposed reforms. The media coverage was extensive, with journalists highlighting the significance of the changes and the impact they would have on the city's governance.

One of the most impactful reforms was the establishment of an independent anti-corruption commission. This commission, composed of respected legal experts, community leaders, and former law enforcement officials, was tasked with investigating and prosecuting cases of corruption within the government and the private sector.

At the inauguration ceremony for the commission, David stood alongside key allies, addressing a crowd of supporters and media representatives.

"Today marks a historic moment in our fight for justice and integrity," David said, his voice filled with conviction. "The establishment of this independent anti-corruption commission is a critical step toward ensuring that our government remains transparent and accountable to the people it serves. This commission will have the authority to investigate and prosecute cases of corruption, holding those who abuse their power accountable. Together, we can build a city that is fair, just, and prosperous for everyone."

The applause was deafening, and David felt a deep sense of fulfillment. The journey had been challenging, but moments like this reaffirmed his commitment to the cause.

Despite the ongoing attacks from the Power Brokers, David's administration continued to make strides in advancing their reform agenda. The collapse of the Power Brokers' network was accelerating, with more high-profile arrests and indictments making headlines.

One evening, as David was reviewing the latest developments with Rachel and Tom, he received a call from Emily Reyes.

"David, I've got more information," Emily said, her voice urgent. "We've uncovered additional evidence that links several key figures in the Power Brokers' network to illegal activities, including money laundering and bribery. This could be the final piece we need to bring them down."

David felt a surge of hope. "Thank you, Emily. Your work has been invaluable. We'll use this information to strengthen our case and ensure that justice is served."

As the investigation continued, David and his team worked closely with law enforcement to trace financial transactions, gather testimonies, and build a comprehensive case against the Power Brokers' network. The evidence they uncovered was damning, and the public's demand for action grew louder.

The collapse of the Power Brokers' empire was becoming increasingly apparent. High-profile arrests and indictments made headlines, and the once-powerful network began to unravel. The public rallies, town hall meetings, and community events continued, with people from all walks of life joining the movement for reform.

One of the movement's most significant achievements came in the form of a campaign to address the city's environmental challenges. David's team worked with environmental organizations, community leaders, and local businesses to develop a comprehensive plan to reduce pollution, increase green spaces, and promote sustainable practices.

At a press conference announcing the environmental plan, David stood alongside Sarah Thompson, Carlos Mendoza, and other key allies. The room was filled with community members, activists, and journalists who had fought tirelessly for this reform.

"Today marks a significant step forward in our fight for environmental justice," David said, his voice filled with pride. "This plan is the result of months of hard work and collaboration with our community. It will ensure that our city remains a healthy and sustainable place for future generations. It's a testament to what we can achieve when we come together to fight for what's right."

The applause was thunderous, and David felt a deep sense of fulfillment. The journey had been challenging, but moments like this reaffirmed his commitment to the cause.

Despite the ongoing attacks from the Power Brokers, David's administration continued to make strides in advancing their reform agenda. The collapse of the Power Brokers' network was accelerating, with more high-profile arrests and indictments making headlines.

One evening, as David was reviewing the latest developments with Rachel and Tom, he received a call from Emily Reyes.

"David, I've got more information," Emily said, her voice urgent. "We've uncovered additional evidence that links several key figures in the Power Brokers' network to illegal activities, including money laundering and bribery. This could be the final piece we need to bring them down."

David felt a surge of hope. "Thank you, Emily. Your work has been invaluable. We'll use this information to strengthen our case and ensure that justice is served."

As the investigation continued, David and his team worked closely with law enforcement to trace financial transactions, gather testimonies, and build a comprehensive case against the Power Brokers' network. The evidence they uncovered was damning, and the public's demand for action grew louder.

The collapse of the Power Brokers' empire was becoming increasingly apparent. High-profile arrests and indictments made headlines, and the once-powerful network began to unravel. The public rallies, town hall meetings, and community events continued, with people from all walks of life joining the movement for reform.

One of the movement's most significant achievements came in the form of a campaign to address the city's environmental challenges. David's team worked with environmental organizations, community leaders, and local businesses to develop a comprehensive plan to reduce pollution, increase green spaces, and promote sustainable practices.

At a press conference announcing the environmental plan, David stood alongside Sarah Thompson, Carlos Mendoza, and other key allies. The room was filled with community members, activists, and journalists who had fought tirelessly for this reform.

"Today marks a significant step forward in our fight for environmental justice," David said, his voice filled with pride. "This plan is the result of months of hard work and collaboration with our community. It will ensure that our city remains a healthy and sustainable place for future generations. It's a testament to what we can achieve when we come together to fight for what's right."

The applause was thunderous, and David felt a deep sense of fulfillment. The journey had been challenging, but moments like this reaffirmed his commitment to the cause.

Despite the ongoing attacks from the Power Brokers, David's administration continued to make strides in advancing their reform agenda. The public's demand for accountability and transparency was stronger than ever, and the collapse of the Power Brokers' network was accelerating.

One evening, as David sat in his office reflecting on the journey so far, Rachel walked in with a smile on her face. "David, I have good news. The investigation into the Power Brokers is progressing, and several key members have been indicted. The tide is turning."

David felt a sense of relief and accomplishment. The battle was far from over, but they had made significant progress. "That's fantastic news, Rachel. We've come a long way, and we're making a real difference."

Rachel nodded, her eyes filled with determination. "We have, and we will continue to fight. This city deserves a government that truly serves its people. And we're going to make sure that happens."

David smiled, feeling a renewed sense of purpose. The journey had been challenging, and there were undoubtedly more obstacles ahead. But he knew that they were on the right path. The collapse of the Power Brokers' empire was a testament to the power of truth and the resilience of the human spirit.

As David looked out over the city once more, he felt a sense of hope. The skyline, once a symbol of ambition and burden, now represented the potential for genuine change. He had made a promise to the people, and he was determined to see it through.

The battle against the Power Brokers had tested his resolve and his principles, but David Collins was ready to face the challenges ahead. With the support of his allies and the community, he would continue to fight for a city that truly served its people. The path was clear, and the future looked brighter than ever before.

Chapter 15: The New Era

The morning sun rose over the city, casting a warm, golden glow across the skyline. The atmosphere was filled with a sense of renewal and hope. David Collins stood in his office, gazing out at the city that had become the symbol of his struggle and triumph. The journey had been long and fraught with challenges, but now, as the newly elected leader of a reformed administration, David felt a profound sense of purpose and optimism.

The collapse of the Power Brokers' empire had paved the way for a new era of transparency, justice, and genuine public service. The people had rallied around David's vision for a better future, and the public demand for accountability had led to sweeping changes in the political landscape. David's administration was now at the forefront of a movement that promised to transform the city and inspire similar efforts across the nation.

David's thoughts were interrupted by a knock on the door. Rachel entered, her face radiant with excitement.

"David, the inauguration ceremony is about to begin," she said. "The crowd is already gathering, and the atmosphere is electric. This is the moment we've all been working toward."

David smiled, feeling a surge of gratitude and pride. "Thank you, Rachel. Let's make this a day to remember."

The inauguration ceremony was held in the heart of the city, in a grand plaza surrounded by historic buildings and lush gardens. Thousands of people had gathered to witness the event, their faces filled with hope and anticipation. The stage was adorned with banners and flags, symbolizing the unity and determination of the community.

As David took the stage, the crowd erupted into applause. He stood at the podium, flanked by his family, key allies, and newly appointed members of his administration. The moment was filled with emotion, as David looked out at the sea of faces and felt the weight of their expectations.

"Good morning," David began, his voice resonating with conviction. "Today marks the beginning of a new era for our city. We have come together to build a future that is fair, just, and prosperous for everyone. Our journey has been challenging, but we have emerged stronger and more united than ever."

He paused, letting his words sink in. "Over the past months, we have exposed corruption, held those responsible accountable, and laid the groundwork for lasting change. But our work is far from over. Today, we reaffirm our commitment to transparency, justice, and genuine public service. We will govern with integrity, putting the needs of the people above all else."

The crowd erupted into applause once more, their support and enthusiasm palpable. David continued, outlining the key principles that would guide his administration and the specific measures they would take to achieve their goals.

"Transparency will be the cornerstone of our administration," David said. "We will ensure that all government actions and decisions are open to public scrutiny. We will implement strict regulations on campaign financing, independent oversight of public contracts, and enhanced protections for whistleblowers. Our government will be accountable to the people it serves."

He went on to discuss the importance of justice and equality, emphasizing the need to address systemic issues and create opportunities for all citizens.

"Justice is not just about punishing wrongdoing—it's about creating a society where everyone has the opportunity to thrive," David said. "We will work tirelessly to address disparities in education, healthcare, housing, and employment. We will promote policies that ensure equal access to resources and opportunities, and we will support initiatives that uplift marginalized communities."

David's speech was met with overwhelming approval from the crowd. He could see the hope and determination in their eyes, and he knew that they were ready to embark on this journey with him.

As the ceremony continued, David introduced the members of his new administration, each of whom had been chosen for their commitment to integrity and public service. The team was diverse, representing a wide range of backgrounds and expertise, but they were united by a shared vision for the future.

"Together, we will lead this city into a new era of transparency, justice, and genuine public service," David said. "Our administration is dedicated to serving the people and building a better future for all. We are ready to face the challenges ahead, and we are confident that, with your support, we can achieve great things."

The inauguration ceremony concluded with a sense of unity and optimism. The crowd dispersed, but the energy and excitement lingered in the air. David and his team returned to City Hall, ready to begin the hard work of governing and implementing their ambitious agenda.

Over the next few weeks, the new administration hit the ground running. They prioritized transparency by making government records and meetings accessible to the public. They launched a comprehensive audit of public contracts and expenditures, ensuring that all transactions were conducted with integrity and accountability.

The independent anti-corruption commission, established during David's previous term, continued its work with renewed vigor. The commission's investigations led to additional arrests and prosecutions, further dismantling the remnants of the Power Brokers' network and restoring public trust in the government.

David's administration also focused on addressing the systemic issues that had plagued the city for years. They implemented policies to improve education, healthcare, and housing, working closely with community leaders and organizations to ensure that their efforts were effective and inclusive.

One of the most significant initiatives was the creation of a citywide task force on education reform. This task force, composed of educators, parents, students, and community leaders, developed a comprehensive plan to improve the quality of education in public schools. The plan included increased funding for schools, expanded access to early childhood education, and programs to support students' mental health and well-being.

At a press conference announcing the education reform plan, David stood alongside members of the task force, addressing a room filled with journalists, educators, and community members.

"Education is the foundation of our future," David said, his voice filled with conviction. "We must ensure that every child in our city has access to a high-quality education. This plan is the result of extensive collaboration with educators, parents, and community leaders, and it represents a significant investment in our children's future."

The response from the public was overwhelmingly positive. Parents and educators praised the administration's commitment to improving education, and students expressed hope for a brighter future. The media coverage was extensive, highlighting the significance of the reforms and the impact they would have on the city's education system.

David's administration also made significant strides in addressing healthcare disparities. They worked with healthcare providers, community organizations, and policymakers to develop initiatives aimed at increasing access to quality healthcare for all residents. These initiatives included expanding community health centers, providing affordable health insurance options, and implementing programs to address mental health and substance abuse issues.

One of the most impactful healthcare initiatives was the creation of a mobile health clinic program. These clinics, staffed by medical professionals and equipped with essential medical supplies, traveled to underserved neighborhoods to provide free healthcare services to residents.

At the launch of the mobile health clinic program, David stood alongside healthcare providers and community leaders, addressing a crowd of supporters and media representatives.

"Access to quality healthcare is a fundamental right," David said, his voice filled with passion. "We must ensure that all residents, regardless of their circumstances, have access to the healthcare services they need. This mobile health clinic program is a critical step toward achieving that goal. It will bring essential healthcare services directly to our communities, ensuring that no one is left behind."

The response from the public was overwhelmingly positive. Residents praised the administration's efforts to address healthcare disparities, and healthcare providers expressed their commitment to serving the community. The media coverage was extensive, highlighting the significance of the mobile health clinic program and its impact on the city's healthcare system.

David's administration also focused on addressing the city's affordable housing crisis. They worked with local developers, nonprofits, and community leaders to create a comprehensive plan that included the construction of new affordable housing units, rental assistance programs, and measures to prevent displacement due to gentrification.

At a press conference announcing the affordable housing plan, David stood alongside housing advocates and community leaders, addressing a room filled with journalists, residents, and supporters.

"Everyone deserves a safe and affordable place to call home," David said, his voice resonating with conviction. "This affordable housing plan is the result of months of hard work and collaboration with our community. It will ensure that everyone in our city has access to affordable housing and that our neighborhoods remain vibrant and diverse. It's a testament to what we can achieve when we come together to fight for what's right."

The response from the public was overwhelmingly positive. Residents praised the administration's commitment to addressing the housing crisis, and housing advocates expressed their support for the plan. The media coverage was extensive, highlighting the significance of the affordable housing plan and its impact on the city's housing market.

As David's administration continued to implement their ambitious agenda, they remained focused on transparency, justice, and genuine public service. They worked closely with community leaders, organizations, and residents to ensure that their efforts were effective and inclusive.

One of the most significant achievements of David's administration was the creation of a citywide initiative to promote civic engagement and community involvement. This initiative, known as "Together We Rise," aimed to empower residents to take an active role in shaping the future of their city.

At the launch of the "Together We Rise" initiative, David stood alongside community leaders and residents, addressing a room filled with journalists, activists, and supporters.

"Together, we can build a city that is fair, just, and prosperous for everyone," David said, his voice filled with hope. "The 'Together We Rise' initiative is about empowering residents to take an active role in shaping the future of our city. It's about fostering a sense of community and collaboration, and ensuring that everyone's voice is heard. Together, we can achieve great things."

The response from the public was overwhelmingly positive. Residents praised the administration's efforts to promote civic engagement and community involvement, and activists expressed their support for the initiative.

The media coverage was extensive, highlighting the significance of the "Together We Rise" initiative and its impact on the city's civic landscape.

As David's administration continued to make strides in advancing their reform agenda, they remained focused on their core principles of transparency, justice, and genuine public service. They worked tirelessly to address systemic issues, promote equality, and create opportunities for all residents.

One evening, as David sat in his office reflecting on the journey so far, Rachel walked in with a smile on her face. "David, I have good news. The latest polls show that public support for our administration is at an all-time high. People are seeing the positive impact of our reforms, and they believe in our vision for the future."

David felt a sense of relief and accomplishment. The journey had been challenging, but they had made significant progress. "That's fantastic news, Rachel. We've come a long way, and we're making a real difference."

Rachel nodded, her eyes filled with determination. "We have, and we will continue to fight. This city deserves a government that truly serves its people. And we're going to make sure that happens."

David smiled, feeling a renewed sense of purpose. The journey had been challenging, and there were undoubtedly more obstacles ahead. But he knew that they were on the right path. The new era of transparency, justice, and genuine public service was a testament to the power of truth and the resilience of the human spirit.

As David looked out over the city once more, he felt a sense of hope. The skyline, once a symbol of ambition and burden, now represented the potential for genuine change. He had made a promise to the people, and he was determined to see it through.

The battle against the Power Brokers had tested his resolve and his principles, but David Collins was ready to face the challenges ahead. With the support of his allies and the community, he would continue to fight for a city that truly served its people. The path was clear, and the future looked brighter than ever before.

In the months that followed, David's administration continued to build on their successes. They introduced new policies to promote economic development, support small businesses, and create jobs. They launched initiatives to improve public transportation, enhance public safety, and protect the environment.

One of the most significant initiatives was the creation of a citywide task force on economic development. This task force, composed of business leaders, economists, and community representatives, developed a comprehensive plan to stimulate economic growth and create opportunities for all residents.

At a press conference announcing the economic development plan, David stood alongside members of the task force, addressing a room filled with journalists, business leaders, and community members.

"Economic development is essential for the prosperity of our city," David said, his voice filled with conviction. "We must ensure that all residents have access to good jobs, affordable housing, and quality services. This economic development plan is the result of extensive collaboration with business leaders, economists, and community representatives. It represents a significant investment in our city's future."

The response from the public was overwhelmingly positive. Business leaders praised the administration's commitment to economic development, and residents expressed hope for a brighter future. The media coverage was extensive, highlighting the significance of the economic development plan and its impact on the city's economy.

David's administration also made significant strides in improving public transportation. They worked with transportation experts, community leaders, and policymakers to develop initiatives aimed at expanding public transit options, reducing traffic congestion, and promoting sustainable transportation practices.

One of the most impactful transportation initiatives was the creation of a citywide bike-sharing program. This program, designed to provide affordable and accessible transportation options for residents, included the installation of bike-sharing stations throughout the city and the development of dedicated bike lanes.

At the launch of the bike-sharing program, David stood alongside transportation experts and community leaders, addressing a crowd of supporters and media representatives.

"Access to affordable and sustainable transportation is essential for the well-being of our city," David said, his voice filled with passion. "We must ensure that all residents have access to reliable and convenient transportation options. This bike-sharing program is a critical step toward achieving that goal. It will provide residents with an affordable and eco-friendly way to get around the city."

The response from the public was overwhelmingly positive. Residents praised the administration's efforts to improve public transportation, and transportation experts expressed their support for the bike-sharing program. The media coverage was extensive, highlighting the significance of the program and its impact on the city's transportation system.

David's administration also focused on enhancing public safety. They worked with law enforcement agencies, community organizations, and policymakers to develop initiatives aimed at reducing crime, improving emergency response times, and fostering trust between the police and the community.

One of the most significant public safety initiatives was the creation of a community policing program. This program, designed to build trust and collaboration between law enforcement and the community, included the implementation of community policing strategies, increased officer training, and the establishment of community advisory boards.

At the launch of the community policing program, David stood alongside law enforcement officials and community leaders, addressing a crowd of supporters and media representatives.

"Public safety is a fundamental right for all residents," David said, his voice filled with conviction. "We must ensure that our city is safe and secure for everyone. This community policing program is a critical step toward achieving that goal. It will foster trust and collaboration between law enforcement and the community, ensuring that everyone's voice is heard."

The response from the public was overwhelmingly positive. Residents praised the administration's efforts to enhance public safety, and law enforcement officials expressed their support for the community policing program. The media coverage was extensive, highlighting the significance of the program and its impact on the city's public safety.

As David's administration continued to make strides in advancing their reform agenda, they remained focused on their core principles of transparency, justice, and genuine public service. They worked tirelessly to address systemic issues, promote equality, and create opportunities for all residents.

One evening, as David sat in his office reflecting on the journey so far, Rachel walked in with a smile on her face. "David, I have good news. The latest polls show that public support for our administration is at an all-time high. People are seeing the positive impact of our reforms, and they believe in our vision for the future."

David felt a sense of relief and accomplishment. The journey had been challenging, but they had made significant progress. "That's fantastic news, Rachel. We've come a long way, and we're making a real difference."

Rachel nodded, her eyes filled with determination. "We have, and we will continue to fight. This city deserves a government that truly serves its people. And we're going to make sure that happens."

David smiled, feeling a renewed sense of purpose. The journey had been challenging, and there were undoubtedly more obstacles ahead. But he knew that they were on the right path. The new era of transparency, justice, and genuine public service was a testament to the power of truth and the resilience of the human spirit.

As David looked out over the city once more, he felt a sense of hope. The skyline, once a symbol of ambition and burden, now represented the potential for genuine change. He had made a promise to the people, and he was determined to see it through.

The battle against the Power Brokers had tested his resolve and his principles, but David Collins was ready to face the challenges ahead. With the support of his allies and the community, he would continue to fight for a city that truly served its people. The path was clear, and the future looked brighter than ever before.

Don't miss out!

Visit the website below and you can sign up to receive emails whenever Nicholas Andrew Martinez publishes a new book. There's no charge and no obligation.

https://books2read.com/r/B-A-HUIXB-PNXIF

BOOKS2READ

Connecting independent readers to independent writers.

About the Author

Nicholas Andrew Martinez is a distinguished author known for his gripping political fiction. His novels delve into the intricacies of power, corruption, and intrigue, offering readers a thrilling and insightful look at the political landscape. With a background in political science and a passion for storytelling, Martinez crafts narratives that are both thought-provoking and suspenseful. Outside of writing, he enjoys analyzing current events, traveling, and engaging in civic discussions. Nicholas's work continues to captivate and challenge readers, cementing his reputation as a leading voice in political fiction.

Milton Keynes UK
Ingram Content Group UK Ltd.
UKHW042038031224
452078UK00001B/233